Snapped

An Agent Jade Monroe FBI Crime Thriller
Book 1

C. M. Sutter

AUTHOR'S NOTE

This book is a work of fiction by C. M. Sutter. Names, characters, places, and incidents are products of the author's imagination or are used solely for entertainment. Any resemblance to actual events or persons, living or dead, is entirely coincidental.

The scanning, uploading, and distribution of this book via the Internet or any other means without the permission of the publisher is illegal and punishable by law. Please purchase only authorized electronic editions, and do not participate in or encourage electronic piracy of copyrighted materials. Your support of the author's rights is appreciated.

ABOUT THE AUTHOR

C.M. Sutter is a crime fiction writer who resides in the Midwest, although she is originally from California.

She is a member of numerous writers' organizations, including Fiction for All, Fiction Factor, and Writers etc.

In addition to writing, she enjoys spending time with her family and dog. She is an art enthusiast and loves to create handmade objects. Gardening, hiking, bicycling, and traveling are a few of her favorite pastimes. Be the first to be notified of new releases and promotions at: http://cmsutter.com.

C.M. Sutter

http://cmsutter.com/

Snapped:
An Agent Jade Monroe FBI Crime Thriller, Book 1

Murder happens in Houston, but when the most recent murders take on disturbing similarities, local law enforcement officers fear a serial killer is roaming their streets.

Former sheriff's department sergeant Jade Monroe has just graduated from the FBI's serial crimes unit in homicide and is called to Houston with her partner, J.T. Harper, to take on her first assignment—apprehending the person responsible for these gruesome crimes.

With victims piling up and the clock ticking, Jade and J.T. need to intensify their search because there's no sign the killer is slowing down.

After a late-night epiphany while she's alone, Jade suddenly comes face to face with the killer, and now Jade is missing. The clock continues to tick—but this time it's for her.

Stay abreast of each new book release by signing up for my VIP e-mail list at:

http://cmsutter.com/newsletter/

Find more books in the Jade Monroe Series here:

http://cmsutter.com/available-books/

Chapter 1

He had to be the first to die—it was only fitting. After all, Ted Arneson's mistakes had initiated the domino effect that turned a typical afternoon into Jordan's worst nightmare.

She had followed him for days and knew his every movement. She was in the next booth at Finley's when Ted took his wife, Amanda, out to dinner. And during the rainstorm last Tuesday, Jordan was right behind the couple and their daughter, Megan, as they stood in line at the grocery store. Staying within earshot helped Jordan plan her revenge. She wouldn't be happy until every person responsible was checked off her list and dead.

She sat in the driver's seat of her dark blue Accord and drummed the steering wheel with her well-manicured nails. Nervousness had set in and made her squirm with anticipation, but she was excited nonetheless. Six months to the day had gone by, and it was time. Jordan watched from a half block away, her car tucked neatly behind a wide tree. Today, Amanda and the daughter were leaving town for an extended visit with the child's grandparents. Jordan had Ted all to herself.

She tore away the red cellophane strip on the cigarette pack and peeled back the foil. The cancer sticks stood neatly side by side like sardines packed in a tin can. She pulled the first one out with her long nails and slipped it between her lips. With the lighter grasped in her hand and her thumb on the roller wheel, Jordan gave a quick flick that sent a small burst of fire out the tip. The cigarette's end sizzled and turned orange when it touched the flame. She sucked in that first long drag.

Movement at the Arneson house caught her eye, and Jordan's back stiffened. She sat up straight, her eyes laser focused as the garage door rose. Amanda, holding the child's hand, walked out first. The lift gate on the SUV sprang open when she clicked the key fob. Suitcases appeared to weigh Ted's arms down as he approached the vehicle and tossed them in the back. He slammed the gate, secured the child in the car seat, and kissed his wife goodbye.

Isn't that sweet? Too bad it's the last time they'll ever see you alive.

Jordan turned the key in the ignition and pressed the window button on her armrest. Ribbons of smoke streamed out into the October air. She took another deep draw on the cigarette and held her position as the family waved their goodbyes and Amanda backed out of the driveway. Once Ted had returned to the house, Jordan shifted the car into Drive and crept forward. She'd stay far enough back to avoid detection, and with all day to plan her move, she wasn't pressed for time. Jordan followed Amanda out of their suburban neighborhood and all the way to the airport on the northeast side of Houston. She had to be confident that the wife and daughter were long gone. What she had planned for Ted later would definitely take some time.

With a last-second turn, Jordan pulled into a gas station directly across from the Airport Shuttle and Speedy Park. When she saw the flash of the left taillight of Amanda's SUV, she shifted into Park and waited. Within minutes, Jordan caught a glimpse of Amanda and the daughter boarding the shuttle. The driver took their bags and loaded them, and they were whisked away. With a final look at the van heading toward the departures area, Jordan felt confident enough to continue with her plan. She sped away and drove the twenty-minute freeway route to the Store-All facility where everything she needed to complete her tasks was in a sixteen-by-twenty-five-foot storage unit. With a click of her left-hand blinker, Jordan pulled into the driveway and stopped at the gate. She slid her key card into the slot, the arm lifted, and she pulled in. Her storage space was in Row C. Unit 66 was at the far end, right where she liked it, and the spot afforded her the privacy she needed. She parked the car alongside the garage and killed the engine then rounded her vehicle, pulled the brass-colored key out of her pocket, and turned it in the lock. With the door latch in her right hand, she lifted the roller door and clicked on the light. Inside sat a white cargo van. She opened its double back doors and stepped in. Everything she needed had been loaded in the back a week prior, but double-checking couldn't hurt. With a smile of satisfaction, Jordan slammed the doors, climbed inside, and backed out.

She pulled her car in to fill the vacated space then lowered the garage door, locked it, and gave the handle a strong tug to make sure it was secure. She looked forward to the cover of darkness, when Ted would be relaxing at home—all alone. She'd make sure he'd have a slow, painful death and get everything he deserved. Jordan lit another cigarette, cranked up the music, and headed home.

Chapter 2

It felt good to finally be home. After four months of specialized training in the FBI's Serial Homicide Division in Quantico, I had arrived back in North Bend late last night and would begin my new position with the FBI tomorrow morning. I had to thank Dave Spencer for expediting my entry into that intense training program. I was now part of the special unit in serial homicide crimes at the new regional office right in Milwaukee. The location was a godsend.

My mind was clear, I had a new focus, and I would push forward to help apprehend the worst serial killers, including my dad's murderer. I didn't care what the end result would be in that case—dead or alive, preferably dead, was fine with me. I wanted Max Sims off the streets so he couldn't kill another innocent person.

That fall day was cool and sunny. Autumn leaves crunched under our feet as my sister, Amber, and I walked to the gravesite. A slight breeze found its way down the collar of my jacket and made me shiver. I pulled the zipper up higher—I'd never been a fan of the cold. With a swipe across the stone, I brushed the leaves off the granite memorial, and we took our places on the grass. My fingers outlined his name—Thomas Charles Monroe—carved deeply in the stone. Amber pulled up a blade of grass and positioned it between her thumb knuckles. She cupped her hand and blew over the single strip of grass. A deep birdlike call sounded. Her eyes twinkled with happiness, but tears quickly pooled in her lower lids.

"I can still do it, Daddy. You taught me how to do that when I was seven years old, and I still have the knack."

I squeezed her hand. "Dad is laughing right now, you know. You've always made him happy, hon."

Amber checked the time on her cell phone and sighed deeply. "Come on. Jack and Kate are meeting us in ten minutes." She held out her hand and pulled me up.

With a heavy heart and a prayer, we said goodbye to our dad and told him how much we loved and missed him. Amber positioned the bouquet of flowers perfectly under his name, then we each placed a small pebble on his gravestone—a symbol that someone had been there to visit. With my arm around her shoulder, Amber and I turned and walked back to the car.

We met up with Jack and Kate at Joey's Bar and Grill. A round of welcome-home hugs and kisses made me feel happy and loved by the best friends I could ever hope to have. Inside, at a cozy corner bar table, we ordered our beers and browsed the latest additions to the menu.

I leaned in, my chin propped in my hands and my elbows on the table. "I want to hear everything that's going on, guys. I hate being out of the loop."

Jack began by saying how different it was to have Horbeck as his new partner. Horbeck was a bit more predictable than I was, which made things somewhat dull. A round of laughter erupted as we clanked our beer mugs against each other's.

"You didn't hear that from me, though." Jack chuckled. "It's good to have you home, Jade. It's like something was missing in our lives for the past four months."

"No kidding, dork, it was *me.*" I gave him a playful punch to the shoulder. "Seriously, though, thanks for the sweet words, partner. I guess you're stuck with that title. You'll always be my partner, even if it's only to catch up or share information on cases." I looked from face to face. "No sightings or chatter coming in anymore?"

They all knew what I meant—I didn't need to mention his name.

"Sorry, but no," Kate said as she redirected the conversation. "So what do you think? Amber and I are deputies now. Pretty sweet, huh?"

I knew she was trying to change the subject, bless her heart, and I smiled. "Yeah, that is pretty sweet. You'll have to watch those doughnuts, though. Sitting in a squad car all day setting up speed traps along the highway will quickly give you both fat asses."

Amber shushed me. "Lieutenant Clark said he's going to shake up the department soon."

"What does that mean?"

"I don't know. Move people around would be my guess."

I turned my head. "Jack?"

He nodded. "Sooner or later we were going to need more detectives now that you bailed on us."

"Gee, thanks."

Jack took a sip of his beer. "But seriously, I'm sure he's thinking of staffing the bull pen with a few more people." He jerked his chin toward Kate. "And she has her own specialty as a psychic consultant when the need arises. I'm sure he'll clue us in on his plan soon enough. Anyway, how was Quantico?"

"Crazy cool but intense. Dave Spencer introduced me to a lot of the top dogs in the serial homicide unit. Amber, someday when you join the FBI and train to be a profiler, you'll see exactly what I mean. The main headquarters is in downtown Milwaukee, but the new regional serial homicide division has its own building in Glendale. That'll make my daily drive a bit quicker, plus I won't get tangled up in the Milwaukee gridlock. From what I've been told, they run a lean and mean department. Guess I'll find out firsthand tomorrow."

"What areas of the US do they cover?" Kate asked.

"From what I've been told, this new unit covers the Midwest and the plains states. I'm really excited to get started."

Amber grinned. "Sounds like your kind of people, sis."

"I agree, and I hope I fit in. They already know by my profile that I'm willing to travel whenever and wherever they have to go. Not married, no kids, and I'll always have a 'go bag' packed. I can leave at the drop of a hat."

Jack gave me a concerned look. "Just make sure you're

doing this for the right reason, Jade. I know you want to apprehend Max Sims for your dad's sake, but check yourself daily. You need to be at your best for other people too."

"Thanks, Jack, and you know I will. I've always appreciated your honesty."

After our lunch of burgers and beers, Amber and I left for home. I had more paperwork to go over before Monday, and I hoped to spend some quiet time with her while I had the chance. I knew this new position would have me traveling often to different states, and I wanted to make sure she felt safe and comfortable at home since she would be spending occasional nights alone.

Inside the house, I jiggled the newly installed patio doors and looked over the secondary set of doors carefully. A decorative but highly functional set of wrought-iron security gates fit in front of the glass sliders. They would always be locked as a double precaution unless we were out on the deck. I took a seat at the kitchen table and read through the manual for the high-tech alarm system that was put in right before I left for Quantico. I hadn't had time to read it over until now.

"Do you know everything there is to know about the alarm system, sis?"

"Uh-huh. I read it three times, and if somebody tries to disable it, or the electricity, a signal will go directly to the police station."

"Good. This place will be as secure as Fort Knox soon enough. All we're lacking is a panic room in the basement." I chuckled at Amber's expression. "I'm kidding. You have a big gun, sis. Just make sure it's always within reach. If anyone gets past the security system *and* the locked gate, go ahead and shoot them."

"You know I will."

"Just make sure it isn't a friend or family first. After that, all bets are off." I stood and stretched. "I've got to change the paper in Polly and Porky's cage." I studied Amber's face before I walked away, and saw concern. "Honey, whenever I have to leave for a few days, there's always the option of staying with Mom."

"I know, but I want to be tough and fearless like you, Jade. I'll be damned if I'm going to live my life being afraid like Kate was for so many years."

"Give it time, Amber. I promise it will get better." I glanced at the spot where my dad and the recliner had sat that horrible night four months earlier. I didn't want to dwell on that vision etched in my mind, and I needed to be strong for my sister. I'd never tell her how many nights I cried myself to sleep. I gave Amber a hug then went to my bedroom to tend to my beloved birds.

Chapter 3

That night, Jordan parked the van two blocks from Ted's house and exited the vehicle. She scanned the street when she got out—secluded and dark. At the end of a cul-de-sac devoid of street lamps, she could move about unseen. She rounded the van and opened the back doors. She reached in, grabbed the black backpack she had packed earlier that day, and slung it over her left shoulder. The contents would do the trick and last her several days if necessary.

Ted Arneson was a surveyor by trade, and his miscalculation in the property lines between Jordan's home and her neighbor's was what had started the chain of events that caused the tragedy six months prior. It was time to right the wrong.

Thanks to the moonless night and her black attire, Jordan knew her movements would be virtually invisible as she followed the easement between the lot lines. Most homes had well-lit kitchens and dinettes that faced the back of the house. With the blinds open and a false sense of privacy, nobody could have a clue that fifty feet out, somebody was watching. Jordan knew the route, and once she arrived at the backyards on Ted's street, she counted the houses. His was the sixth from the corner.

She pressed the button that illuminated the face on her wristwatch and checked the time—7:15. She watched for movement in his house as she crept closer. All of the rooms nearest the patio were brightly lit. Since she didn't know the layout of his home, she'd have to be extra cautious as she approached. She assumed that, as with most of the homes she had already passed, those rooms were the dining area, kitchen, and possibly the family room. Jordan reached the patio and breathed a sigh of relief. Patios were quieter than creaky decks, and she could slink along the back side of the house without making noise. She saw movement through the doors—the reflection of the television screen bounced off the glass. Ted was likely in the family room.

Jordan followed the outer wall around the side of the house until she reached the family room window. Through the half-closed blinds, she saw him. Ted was on the recliner and faced the television, his feet up, and he was sound asleep. Once inside, she'd have to quickly subdue him before he had a chance to grab the cell phone on the end table next to him. She was thankful there wasn't a dog in the house. That would definitely throw a wrench in her plans. Ted's home had no alarm, either—she had checked that out a few days back. It was time to go.

Jordan slipped on the rubber gloves that would make gripping the glass patio door easier. The stun gun was already secured in her jacket pocket. With her arms outstretched and her fingers splayed, she lifted the door out of the locking mechanism and slid it to the side, just enough to get through the opening. She waited for the sound of the recliner lever lowering the footrest but heard nothing. She stepped over the threshold and into the dinette then slipped off her shoes and continued forward. The family room was just beyond the kitchen wall, and the drone of the TV would muffle any sound she might accidentally make. Each small step took her closer to the mission she had been anticipating. Jordan reached the wall and peeked around the corner. Ted remained asleep and could have no idea what was coming. With the stun gun in her right hand and her thumb on the red button, she approached him cautiously. His heavy lids opened right at the second she leaned in and gave him the full force of the high-voltage gun to his neck. The scent of scorched skin wafted up her nose as she watched the current bounce back and forth between the prongs. A short involuntary grunt sounded, then Ted fell unconscious.

Jordan dropped her backpack to the floor and unzipped it. She had to move quickly before he woke. She pulled out the zip ties and secured his arms behind his back. The large white ones bound his ankles together. With a foot-long strip of duct tape, she covered his mouth. Within seconds Ted woke to realize he had been rendered helpless. Fear and confusion engulfed his face as he squirmed to no avail. Then he saw her. She sat on the couch ten feet away and stared blankly at him as if she were in a trance. She shook herself out of her thoughts and returned to the moment. Jordan rose and crossed the room.

"You have no idea who I am, do you?"

He moaned through the duct tape and, with bulging eyes, shook his head.

"Yeah, I didn't think so. No accountability, that's the problem these days. I'll be right back. Don't go anywhere." She chuckled as she disappeared around the corner into the kitchen. Jordan rifled through the cabinets as she tried to find the perfect container. "Ah, here we go. This will do the trick." She went back to the family room and scooped up her backpack. She cocked her head at the bound man. "Comfortable, Ted?" She smiled. "I didn't think so."

Back in the kitchen, Jordan mixed the ingredients into the perfect consistency—smooth and thick but not overly thick. More like pancake batter. Ted had plenty of suffering to endure. She didn't want to kill him too soon.

The sound of his cell phone vibrating sent Jordan into the family room again. She picked it up and saw a text had come in from Amanda. She read it aloud.

We're relaxing by the pool, and Megan is being spoiled rotten by Grandma and Grandpa. They send their love. Tomorrow, we'll be at Disney World for the entire day, and Tuesday is Busch Gardens. Call me when you get a chance.

"Isn't that sweet? Apparently I can take my time with you and get really creative. The old lady and kid aren't coming home anytime soon. I'll text a quick response just so we aren't bothered anymore tonight."

With that done, Jordan dropped the cell phone in her jacket pocket and zipped it up then returned to the kitchen. She came around the corner with a pitcher in hand and set it on the coffee table then pulled a length of rope out of her backpack.

"Time to begin, Ted. I'm going to secure you to the recliner really tight so you don't thrash around. Sound good?" He immediately began squirming. "See what I mean? I knew you weren't the type that would go down without a fight."

Jordan wrapped the rope around Ted's chest and the chair several times then moved down to his legs and did the same. A kicking man would make her task more difficult. She lowered the back of the recliner as far as it would go then secured his forehead to the lounger with the tape. Ted couldn't budge.

She stood to the side and assessed her accomplishments. "Yeah, that looks good." She pulled a funnel out of her backpack then ripped the duct tape from Ted's mouth. "Don't worry. I made it thin enough to swallow. You'll get three ounces every few hours, and don't fight me, or I'll have to pinch your nose closed. I guarantee you, you'll swallow this one way or another."

"Who the hell are you, and why are you doing this to me?"

"Retribution. I have to make this right and bring everything back into balance. Right now, the scale is tipped in the favor of you incompetent murderers. Consider me your judge and jury, and you're the first to go."

Jordan jammed the funnel into Ted's mouth and tipped the pitcher. He gurgled and sputtered the gray liquid as she poured.

"There, that's enough for now. That wasn't so bad, was it? Pretty tasteless, right?"

He gasped and coughed as she pulled the funnel from his mouth. "What are you doing? What was that?"

"What difference does it make? You'll get another dose at ten o'clock." She tore off a fresh strip of tape and pressed it across his mouth then checked the doors, drew the blinds, and took a seat on the couch. By morning he would be dead, and his name would be crossed off the list. She had seven more people to go.

Throughout the night, Jordan poured more of the mixture down Ted's throat. He moaned with what she hoped was excruciating pain as his intestines slowly clogged and solidified. By seven a.m., little life remained in him. In the garage, Jordan scoured the shelves and corners as she looked for the perfect instrument to finish him off with. She had to make a personal statement, and she found exactly what she needed in his work vehicle. Back in the house, she filled the bathtub and poured in the ReadyKrete. This time she needed it thick. She stirred the mixture with a baseball bat she'd found in the garage.

Jordan went to the family room and stared at Ted. He was near death. She filled his mouth one last time with the ReadyKrete and sealed the tape over it. She was sure his throat would solidify quickly. She removed the ropes and dragged him to the bathroom, where he lay on the floor. She checked the concoction in the tub—it was the consistency of thick cement. She lowered him into the deep mixture and pushed him down with the baseball bat. The only part of him exposed above the gray sludge was his head. The ReadyKrete would be solid within the hour, and she planned to wait it out. She needed to do one final thing before moving on to the next name on her list. Jordan positioned Ted so his head was resting back on the flat corner of the tub.

"Yeah, that should do it."

She reached for the surveying tripod she had found in his truck. With a violent downward thrust, she embedded the pointed legs into Ted's eyes then pushed his head beneath the solidifying cement crypt. She gathered her backpack and supplies then slipped out the patio doors and disappeared behind the homes.

Chapter 4

"How cool is this, Jade?"

"What's that?" I set my go bag next to the garage door. The logical place for that bag would be in the trunk of my car at all times, but winter wouldn't be kind to hair products and toothpaste—they would freeze solid. I'd keep the bag on the shelf above the washer and dryer when I was at home.

Amber handed me a cup of coffee and motioned for me to take a seat. I double-checked the time. I had a forty-minute drive ahead of me, but I didn't need to leave quite yet. Amber slipped an oven mitt over her hand and pulled a pan of cinnamon rolls out of the oven. I shook my head in amazement.

"I'm not Wonder Woman, Jade. These are the canned ones that just need to be baked."

I laughed. "Give me a couple of those, damn it. They smell delicious. And yes, you are Wonder Woman, in my eyes, anyway." I reached out and pulled two cinnamon rolls out of the pan and dropped them on my plate. "Ow, those suckers are hot!"

"I was going to tell you to be careful, and I haven't even frosted them yet."

I shook my hand and blew on the burn then opened the can of frosting and smeared a knifeful over my rolls.

"Anyway, back to what I was going to say. Isn't it cool that we're both about to leave for our jobs in law enforcement?"

I cautiously bit into a steaming roll. "Yes, it's way cool. I'll admit, I'm a little nervous though. You know, that fear of the unknown when anyone starts a new job."

"Yeah, I already knew everyone at the sheriff's department thanks to you and the years you worked there. Aren't you going to miss everyone, Jade?"

"I already do."

Twenty minutes later, I backed out of the garage with my go bag on the passenger seat. I waved at Amber, who stood in the doorway and gave me a thumbs-up then closed the overhead behind her.

I guess my life is about to turn a new page. Who would have thought that after only five years with the sheriff's department, a job that I loved, I'd move on to bigger and badder criminals?

I reached the city limit sign for Glendale, population 12,980. An upper-middle-class city, Glendale was a suburb of Milwaukee like many others that blended into one another to make the greater metro Milwaukee area.

I listened to the robot voice on my GPS tell me where to turn once I exited the freeway. I knew the building was close.

The voice spoke up. "You have reached your destination."

"Thanks, robot lady." I powered down my phone and double-checked the address. There wasn't a sign in front of the building that stated it was the FBI's Serial Homicide Division, but the address was correct. Maybe they preferred to remain incognito, or possibly the sign hadn't been erected yet. I pulled into the driveway of the newer single-story tan brick building and circled around to the back. The parking lot consisted of twenty parking spaces, ten to my left and ten to my right. They weren't assigned, so I grabbed a random spot and killed the engine. With my bag slung over my shoulder and the new-employee paperwork in my briefcase, I took a deep, cleansing breath, followed the sidewalk around to the front entrance, and pulled open the door that took me into the vestibule. A second set of glass doors lay ahead of me. I gave them a yank, and nothing happened. The jolt of vibrating glass alerted the two women sitting behind a reception counter. One of the women pointed at a keypad at my right. I nodded when I saw a green button beneath a speaker built into the wall. I pressed it. "I'm Jade Monroe reporting in for my first day of work."

I watched as the same lady pressed a button to her left. The door catch released, and I crossed into the foyer of the sparkling new building. The wall ahead of me bore the FBI insignia in blue tile. I couldn't help smiling as I approached the agents at the counter.

"Miss Monroe, welcome to the FBI's Serial Homicide Division. Before anything else, I'll need to see your ID to establish your identity, then we'll create a pass card for you."

"Of course." I pulled my wallet out of my briefcase,

thumbed the laminated card out of the plastic sleeve, and handed it to her. I had no idea what the ladies' names were—they didn't wear visible name tags. I was sure they both had a badge and probably a gun secured somewhere on their clothing.

"If you'd like to take a seat over there"—she pointed at a cluster of chairs that surrounded an oblong coffee table—"SSA Spelling will be out shortly to guide you through orientation. He'll be your immediate supervisor. You'll get your ID back later with your pass card."

"Oh, okay, thank you."

I took a seat on a tweed-patterned guest chair and twiddled my fingers as I waited. Oddly, I felt as I did in junior high school while I sat outside the principal's office and pondered my impending fate. I stared out the window and wondered whether I had acted in haste. Was this really where I belonged?

"Agent Monroe?"

I looked up to see a nice looking gentleman, who seemed to be Dad's age, staring down at me. I quickly stood, held out my hand, and gave him a firm handshake. "It's very nice to meet you, sir."

"And you as well. I'm Supervisory Special Agent Phil Spelling."

I waited as he gave the paperwork in his hand another glance.

"What do you like to be called, Agent Monroe?"

"I guess it depends on how formal everyone is here. Normally, Jade works well for me."

He grinned with perfectly straight white teeth. "Then Jade it is. And no, we aren't formal here."

I relaxed my shoulders and let out my breath slowly. "That's good to know. I'm looking forward to fitting in."

Agent Spelling walked me around the building. The ladies' room was to my left down a long hallway. He mentioned there were lockers inside where I could stash my go bag. He suggested I keep one here and one at home, and he said I should be ready to leave at a moment's notice no matter where I was. I excused myself, went inside, and tucked my bag in a locker. When I joined him back out in the hallway, we continued on. A nice-sized cafeteria with a wall of vending machines and a beverage counter was to my right, where the corridor ended. The rest of the doors were closed. He showed me the way to the exit door that led to the parking lot.

"Nobody uses the front door except the mailman. As soon as your pass card is ready, you'll use that to get in the building right from the parking lot. It works the same as most hotel room card readers with the slot and a green or a red light. Inside the building, you'll swipe your card in front of the bar code reader to gain entrance to any of those closed rooms. All of the pass cards are on elastic lanyards. Most of us wear them around our necks."

"Got it."

"Our forensic team and tech department are stationed in our downtown headquarters. This branch and building has only been open in Milwaukee for three months. All of the agents stationed here originally were at the downtown building. We run a tight ship and deal only with serial adult crimes and homicides in the Midwest and plains states. Other than the cases in Wisconsin, we focus on requests coming in from other state agencies. There are only a few specialized serial homicide units available to travel, so the FBI opened this regional branch to help lighten the load."

"Understood."

"Okay, before you meet your colleagues, let's get your mug shot and prints taken care of for our files. Your paperwork says you've spent four years as a detective at the Washburn County Sheriff's Department and were promoted to sergeant just last year."

"That's correct, sir."

"'Boss' will do just fine, Jade. The paperwork also says you're highly recommended by SSA Dave Spencer."

"That's also correct, boss. He was instrumental in helping me skirt around time frame obstacles."

We entered a small room where an agent waited to fingerprint me and take my mug shot.

Agent Spelling continued. "And you know Dave how?"

"I didn't know him until recently, but he and my dad were close friends. Dave had a vacation home in San Bernardino, and they golfed together quite a bit when Dave was in the area. That's until my dad's knee started acting up." I smiled with the memories of my dad telling me how he'd whop Dave on the golf course every time they went out. I sighed deeply. "Anyway, they were good buddies. I spoke to Dave about the opportunity with the FBI when he came to my dad's funeral. He arranged everything, pulled the right strings, and got me into the next training course."

Agent Spelling paused as if he were thinking. "Wait a minute. Monroe, huh, from North Bend?"

"Yes, boss."

"Your old man wasn't Tom Monroe, was he?"

I grinned. "I'll proudly confirm that, sir, and he was the best captain North Bend and San Bernardino County ever had."

He smiled and shook his head. "I'll be damned. It certainly is a small world. Your old man and I went to the police academy together. I heard about his death, and I wanted to attend the funeral, but we were in Oklahoma on a case. I'm truly sorry for your loss, Jade. Tom Monroe, huh? That man's reputation preceded him wherever he went."

I felt like crying, but I didn't want my new boss to think I was unstable or, worse, off my rocker. I held it in and walked with my shoulders back and my head held a little higher.

"Ready to meet the team?"

"I'm more than ready, boss."

Agent Spelling swiped the bar code on the back of his pass card across the reader on the wall, and we entered a large room with ten desks, each with its own computer. The far end of the room held a table that could seat twenty, likely for brainstorming, and a large map of the United States. The map, mounted to the wall behind the table, was covered with red pushpins.

"This is our situation room. We have other rooms that

serve different purposes. I'll show you them later. Guys, may I have your attention?"

The people in the room, which totaled four, stopped what they were doing and looked up.

"I'd like to introduce you to Jade Monroe. She recently finished her training in serial homicide studies and was recommended to our team by Dave Spencer."

Everyone nodded as if Dave Spencer was an impressive name in the FBI.

"For the last year, Jade's been a sergeant at the Washburn County Sheriff's Department, and the four years prior, she was a detective there." He pointed at each person and told me their names. "To our far left is Cam Jenkins. Next is Valerie Moore, but we call her Val. The handsome dude to her left is J.T. Harper." J.T. waved and shot a heart-stopping grin my way. "And last but not least is Maria Delgado, our most recent recruit from two months back. Maria, you can give Jade the short version of how much you regret joining our team."

The room erupted with laughter. I knew I would fit in perfectly.

Spelling checked the time. "Okay, people, you have thirty minutes to get acquainted, and then I'll be back. I have to assign the person that would be the best fit as a partner for Jade. Go ahead and get to know each other."

Agent Spelling walked out and closed the door at his back. I was on my own, and I knew I was quickly being sized up. Now was my time to be aggressive, witty, and charming. I'd put my best foot forward and win these four people over as amicable coworkers and future great friends.

"Come on over. Let's sit at the table." J.T. led the way, and we all followed. "Okay, you have the floor, Jade."

I felt my face flush and hoped it wasn't obvious. Each of these people had been in my shoes at some point in their life. I quietly took a long breath and began. I reintroduced myself and gave a brief history of my law enforcement involvement in Washburn County. Cam asked why I had originally decided to become a law enforcement officer, and I told the group how my dad instilled those public servant qualities in me at an early age. He had worked in the sheriff's department for thirty-five years.

"And is your dad still an active officer?" Val asked.

I didn't want to tell the horrific story and certainly didn't need a pity party. I only mentioned that he'd passed away four months ago, but until that time, he was active as the captain at the San Bernardino County Sheriff's Department. J.T. raised his brows as if he were ready to ask a question, but I quickly continued on to say that my sister had just started as a deputy at the North Bend Sheriff's Department and eventually wanted to become an FBI profiler.

"That's a very ambitious career choice," Cam said. "Sounds like law enforcement runs in your family."

"It does, and I loved working at the sheriff's department. I had a great group of colleagues that will remain close friends forever. Being locked within county borders does create a lot of challenges, though. I want to get the worst of the worst, no matter where they are, and serial criminals fit that description. That's why I wanted to be a part of this team."

"We're glad you're on board, Jade, and I think you'll fit in great with us," Maria said. "I started at this location two months ago but originally came from the Detroit area. I'm thirty-three, my last name is Delgado, and I live downtown with my grandma. Being the newest member of the group, I can tell you they're all great people to work with. I've never regretted joining this team, no matter what the boss said. He was just giving you a line of bull."

The rest chuckled.

"I'm Cameron Jenkins, but everyone calls me Cam." He gave me a nod. "I'm the senior team member, other than Spelling, and have been with the FBI for nine years. I'm married to a great woman named Liza, we have an eight-year-old son, Kaden, and I live in Mequon." Cam tipped his head to Val.

"I'm Valerie Moore, but Val is what I go by. I'm divorced, have a five-year-old son, Miles, live in a condo a mile away, and have been with the FBI for four years."

"I guess I'll take up the rear as usual," J.T. said with a smirk. "I'm happily single."

Cam booed him, and they all laughed.

"Hey, dude, you're the minority here, other than Spelling. We're all too smart to be married. Anyway, my christened name is John Thomas Harper, I've been with the FBI for six years, and I'm thirty-seven years old."

Maria piped in. "You forgot to mention that you live in Whitefish Bay with your sister, Julie."

He chuckled. "Yeah, yeah, and don't forget her bulldog, Ralph."

The door opened, and Agent Spelling walked through. "How's it going? Has everyone introduced themselves?"

"Yes, and you all sound like a great group. My question is, do I address everyone by their first names, or do—"

J.T. spoke up. "I think I can speak for everyone in saying that here, at the office, we all go by our first names, other than Spelling. He goes by boss."

Agent Spelling grinned and gave J.T. a nod to continue.

"Outside of this building, introductions are by Special Agent, or SA, and the person's last name. Of course, Spelling would be SSA Spelling, as in Supervisory Special Agent Spelling."

"Thanks, I think I've got a handle on it now," I said.

"Okay, grab some coffee and take your seats again. Let's get started. Jade, I'm going to have you shadow the team locally this week so you can see how we operate. First things first, though. I need to assign you a partner."

I waited until everyone was seated. Earlier, we were casually scattered around the table, but now it was for business. I didn't want to grab a place at the table that somebody had claimed long ago.

J.T. noticed and jerked his chin toward an open seat. "Smart lady we have here. Yeah, we're set in our ways. Everyone has a seat, kind of like at the dinner table."

"I assumed so, and I didn't want to step on any toes my first day here."

Spelling's glance went from left to right. "Ready?"

I looked at each person and thought of who I would consider the best fit for me. I knew the decision wasn't mine, and everyone seemed nice, but I was accustomed to having a male partner.

Spelling continued. "Okay, Val and Maria, you're actively working the Adams homicide case from Lake Geneva, right?"

"That's correct, boss, and it should be wrapped up in a few days," Val said.

"No problem. So that leaves Cam and J.T., and I'm leaning toward J.T. simply because he doesn't have any encumbrances."

They all laughed, but I didn't get the joke.

J.T. stood and leaned over the table with his hand outstretched toward me. I shook it because it was there. "Welcome to the team, partner."

"We're partners?"

He grinned. "Looks that way, since neither of us have encumbrances."

Chapter 5

Jordan sat in the van, keeping her eyes peeled for any activity at the building's front door. She had a perfect view of the 9-1-1 call center from across the parking lot. Beverly Grant's shift was scheduled to end soon, and she would walk outside to her last evening on earth.

The plan was set, Jordan was prepared, and she had a few minutes to kill. Jerry Fosco popped into her mind as she waited. The box next to Jerry's name on that yellow sheet of legal paper was already checked off. He was number two, and his death had been slow and agonizing, as they all would be, if time permitted.

Jordan began her seduction of Jerry Monday night at TaTas, a seedy strip club and bar on the worst side of town. She had a job to complete, no matter how disgusting it was, and had followed him there numerous times. She was well aware of his routine. Inside the darkened building, she sauntered to the bar and pulled up the stool next to him. She ordered a shot of Jim Beam for herself and one for him then laid it on thick and flirted shamelessly. Any egocentric man such as Jerry Fosco would feel flattered by a beautiful woman like Jordan. She fawned over him and gave him her full attention.

Eight shots, two beers, and a lot of innuendos got Jerry out into the evening chill, where the cold weather hit him quickly. His intoxication wasn't only from the liquor but also from her whispered promises of things to come. He was ready and willing to leave and clearly had no idea what was about to happen. Jordan dug deep into his front pants pocket and pulled out his car keys. With a double click of the key fob, she followed the sound of the short beep and saw the flashing lights across the bar's parking lot. With the shorter Jerry slumped over her shoulder while the toes of his shoes scraped across the asphalt, she dragged him to the car and dropped him into the passenger seat. The hard zap of the stun gun on his neck silenced him for the time being.

She chuckled at those memories, but when the evening employees at the 9-1-1 call center caught her eye, she knew the time was close. Jordan needed to return her focus to Bev Grant. The workers entered the building, and the door closed behind them. Soon enough, the daytime operators would exit. Fond memories of Jerry would be shelved for the moment.

She had memorized Beverly Grant's daily habits down to the last detail. After following her to and from work since Monday, back and forth to the kids' soccer games, and the usual trips to the grocery store, Jordan was chomping at the bit. She had more names to check off her to-do list, and that incompetent 9-1-1 operator was number three. Beverly had approximately twenty-two minutes to live.

Jordan stared, her eyes unblinking and fixed on the green digital clock in the van as it counted out the minutes—5:58, 5:59. She held her breath—6:00. The time had come, and there was no turning back. She looked forward to it and welcomed it, just as she had with the other two before Beverly.

With the sleeve of her fleece jacket pulled down and balled up over her fist, she wiped away for the second time the fog that clung to the inside of the windshield. She took a long drag off her third cigarette and lowered the window a few inches more. Her focus returned to the front door, where the daytime emergency dispatch operators exited the call center. Jordan's forehead creased with hatred when she saw her.

There you are, you murdering pig.

Beverly Grant stepped out of the building with her five coworkers and crossed the parking lot. They chatted up a storm, just as they had the previous days when Jordan followed that dispatch operator from work to her house. The predictable minute-by-minute schedule of her prey was something Jordan counted on, and so far, it had worked perfectly. Under the baseball cap and sunglasses she used as cover, she watched as Beverly reached her car and climbed in. The woman apparently had no idea what was coming.

Jordan lifted her glasses and brushed away the blur of tears as she sucked in a deep breath. She checked the time again and turned the key in the ignition. With her thumb and index finger, she flicked the cigarette butt out the window—the job at hand needed her full attention. A shiver of cold went up her spine that late October afternoon and circled her neck. With the button on the armrest pressed and the window closed, she pushed the shifter into Drive and lightly touched the gas pedal as the van coasted along the edge of the parking lot. Jordan pulled out onto the street, three car lengths behind Beverly's Buick. They would drive four blocks through town, a half mile on the county highway, and then three final miles on country roads before Beverly would reach the safety of her home. Neither she nor her car would make it that far. What were now loose lug nuts on the back passenger wheel would turn far worse in about twelve minutes—Jordan had made sure of that.

The back tire began to wobble once Beverly picked up speed on that first country road. Jordan remained four car lengths back in case she had to swerve. Nobody else ever passed by at that time of evening, and they didn't that evening, either. Dusk had settled in, and normal people— ones that weren't murderers—had already taken their seats at the dinner table.

The wheel wobbled again, this time severely, throwing the car off kilter. Brake lights flashed, and Beverly pulled to the gravel shoulder.

Perfect. Here we go.

Jordan dropped the stun gun into her coat pocket, slipped on her gloves, and slid the van in behind Beverly's car. Crunching gravel sounded when she slowed to a stop. She pressed the orange hazard button above the radio and killed the engine. She stepped out, slammed the door behind her, and looked both ways.

Nice and quiet.

Jordan called out to the stranded woman as she approached. "Hey, what seems to be the problem? Do you need help?"

Beverly stood at the back of her car and stared at the tilted rear wheel. Her hands firmly planted on her hips gave away her impatience and disgust. She turned toward Jordan in the dimming light and groaned.

"I was hoping you'd be a man. This damn tire is falling off my car, and I have to get home." She headed to the passenger's side door. "I need to call a tow truck right now."

Jordan smirked—her mind had already gone to that dark place. "Hold on a minute. I'm not quite as incapable as you might think. My husband owns a garage and can fix anything. I'm sure he wouldn't mind stopping out here on his way home. He'll get you back on the road in no time."

The woman stopped and turned around. "Really? Can you give him a call?"

"Sure, but first show me the problem so I can explain it to him."

Jordan neared the irritated woman and glanced at the deep ditch only four feet to their backs. It would definitely come in handy.

"Can you point at the problem?"

"Well for God's sake, can't you see it?"

"Sorry, but it *is* getting close to dark."

It took only a second when Beverly bent down with her finger extended and pointed at the lug nuts. Jordan already had a grip on the stun gun as she pulled it out of her pocket.

She ground the electrodes into the back of Beverly's neck and held it firmly against her skin. Sparks sizzled as the current ticked back and forth between the posts. Jordan turned her head and gritted her teeth with satisfaction.

"You stupid bitch, you deserve this pain and a lot more." She kicked Beverly down into the ditch and watched her hit rocks and brush as she rolled. As much as Jordan wanted to enjoy the moment, there wasn't time to spare, being on a public road. She rounded the Buick, opened the driver's side door, and reached in. She clicked off the hazard lights Beverly had turned on, killed the engine, and locked the doors. With all her might, she launched the keys into the bushes on the opposite side of the road. Seconds later, she slid down the ditch where Beverly lay motionless—her adrenaline had already kicked in.

With each of Beverly's wrists grasped tightly in her hands, Jordan heaved and grunted as she dragged the dead weight of the woman deeper into the cover of the brush. She ran back up the hill to the van. Moaning sounded behind her—she had only a few seconds before the woman would be fully awake and fighting back. With the back doors open, Jordan reached in and grabbed a thirty-pound cinder block then rolled it down the hill. She reached Beverly right as the woman regained consciousness.

Beverly groaned in pain and grabbed at the back of her neck as she tried to right herself. "What happened? Why am I lying on the ground in the weeds?"

"It's where you belong, in the dirt. It's called 'getting what you deserve,' and today is your turn. I'd love to prolong your suffering, but since it's nearly dark and we're in a public place, I don't have the luxury of time. Brace yourself."

Jordan's large frame made lifting the block above her head a doable task—she stood over six feet tall and was as strong as most men. The cinder block crashed down on Beverly Grant's skull with a sickening thud, and the deed was done. Jordan pressed the thumb release on her folding knife and, with a quick swipe, removed the woman's tongue and stomped it into the dirt. With a satisfying glance back, she scampered up the hill, pulled off the bloody gloves, and turned them inside out. She shoved them into her coat pocket, climbed into the van, and sped away. A final check of the time told her the task was completed quickly and efficiently. Her wheels hit the blacktop at 6:20 p.m.

The drive to the storage facility didn't take long, and once Jordan arrived she slid the card into the slot to raise the gate. She drove slowly through to her unit and swapped out the van for her car then continued home. She pulled into the driveway and safely tucked the car into the garage, killed the engine, and climbed out. She sucked in a deep breath for composure and slapped at the wall switch. The overhead door lowered. Stale cigarette odors filled her nose as she passed through the laundry room and into the kitchen. Kent wouldn't be too happy about that. With a twist of her wrist, she cranked open the window above the sink, turned the gas stovetop burner to a low setting, and glanced at the clock. The text she had received from Kent earlier said to expect him home around seven fifteen.

With the plastic container from the refrigerator and a wooden spoon in hand, Jordan quickly scraped the spaghetti and meatballs she had prepared in advance into a stainless steel saucepan and placed it on the burner. Kent would be walking through the door any second. She set the wooden cutting board on the island and began chopping head lettuce for a tossed salad. The front door opened minutes later.

Kent Taylor entered the kitchen and planted an absentminded kiss on his wife's cheek.

"I'm beat. That was ten days from hell. I can't even count the number of doctors that made me wait more than an hour for an appointment that was already set up in advance."

"You make big money being a drug rep and have to expect tough weeks once in a while. I'm beat too, you know."

The look of pity and disgust filled his eyes. Jordan wanted to slap the expression right off his face.

"Why would you be tired? You don't do anything except mope around. That medication is supposed to improve your disposition and depression."

Jordan's skin warmed with red-hot anger. She felt it climb up her chest and neck. Pieces of lettuce fell to the floor as she chopped harder and faster. The knife was a flurry of movement and dangerously close to her fingertips as her face contorted with anger.

"Jordan! Put the damn knife down before you cut yourself." He rubbed his forehead and stared. "Take your damn meds, for crissakes."

"You'd be happy if I was a stoned zombie all the time, wouldn't you? Then you could ignore me more than you already do." She spat the hateful words at him. "The pills don't help, anyway!"

"Then find something that does." Kent unscrewed the top of the whiskey bottle that had a permanent home on the kitchen counter. He tipped it over the rocks glass and poured the amber liquid until the glass was half full. He cursed under his breath as he turned his back toward her and walked away.

Jordan sank the tip of the knife into the cutting board. "What did you just say?"

"I said I'm going to change clothes and wash up."

She heard his shoes clack on the hardwood hallway floor until he reached the carpeted bedroom.

I did find something that helps quite a bit, thank you. At least I'm not drowning my sorrows in a bottle of whiskey.

Later, at bedtime, Kent mentioned he was leaving again first thing in the morning. Stopping back at home between routes was a common occurrence. Being a national sales rep for a drug company kept him on the road more often than he was home.

Jordan lay in bed and thought about the next name on her list.

Chapter 6

I had been out with the group most of the week, working local cases with the downtown headquarters. I was learning the ropes and becoming comfortable with my colleagues. I felt J.T. and I would become great partners, just as Jack and I had been.

I entered the building at seven forty-five Thursday morning with my travel mug in hand. We began each day in the situation room. Either we'd have local cases to help out on or there would be news of some other branch of law enforcement that requested our assistance. We took our seats, had our notepads and pens ready, and waited for SSA Spelling to begin.

"Good morning, guys."

We responded with a round of good mornings back to him.

"I've just received word that the Houston field office would like our assistance. They don't have a serial homicides unit in house, and they're in our district. Here's the information that was passed on to me an hour ago." He took a sip of water and proceeded with the notes he had in front of him. "Apparently over the last week, several murders have taken place throughout the greater Houston area, which in itself isn't unusual. The police department thought there were enough similarities to consult with the Houston field office once the count had reached three. With the FBI's help, they've concluded the murders could be the work of one killer. Of course, until they compared notes from every scene, the city boys were treating the homicides as typical and individual. Now, with more eyes reviewing the police reports, they've realized there is a common connection between all of them."

"What is that connection, boss?" I asked.

"As strange as it sounds, and believe me, I've heard almost everything, these murders have some form of cement in common. Two of the three also had body parts removed."

"Odd," Val said. "Normally the removal of a body part has a significant meaning. I wonder why all three weren't treated the same way."

Cam scratched his head. "Cement is a unique one. Did they expand on the details?"

Spelling looked at his notes again. "Yep, as a matter of fact they did. This unsub is quite creative. Apparently, the first victim was found by his wife a few days ago after coming home from a short trip to Florida with their daughter. Her whereabouts were already confirmed, and she isn't considered a suspect at the moment. Her husband was found entombed in a bathtub of cement. According to the autopsy report, his esophagus, stomach, and intestines had been filled with the product and were blown out."

"He was forced to ingest it?" I asked.

"It appears so. The man was a surveyor by trade, and his eyes had been speared with his work tripod. Pretty gruesome stuff for a wife and child to come home to."

J.T. spoke up. "What about the others?"

"The second man was single and a bricklayer. He was also found in his home. His head was crushed by a cinder block, and his hands were mangled beyond recognition by the garbage disposal."

"Wow, that's vicious. Who found him?" Cam asked.

"Apparently the company he worked for tried to reach him numerous times over the last few days. They finally checked his employee file and found the phone number of his aunt. She had a key to his house and discovered his body."

"If anything is an encumbrance, wouldn't a cinder block be? Why carry something like that around as a murder weapon? Aren't they pretty heavy?" I asked.

"Good question, Jade," Spelling said. "I actually wondered that myself and looked up the answer. Actually, if they're all similar in size, they'd weigh in at close to thirty pounds. A cinder block definitely wouldn't be a convenient murder weapon to lug around."

Maria raised her head after writing down that bit of information. "And the third victim?"

"A 9-1-1 dispatch operator. Wife, mother, regular gal by the interviews conducted with the husband and coworkers. Her vehicle was found abandoned along a road only a few miles from her home early last night. Just this morning, once daylight broke, her body was located hidden among scrub bushes in the same area. Her head had been bashed in with a cinder block, and her tongue had been cut out."

"Wow, that's sending somebody a message," Cam said.

"What about victim connections?" J.T. asked.

"Nothing they've come up with yet. They have a surveyor, a brick layer, and a 9-1-1 operator."

"Tradespeople?" Val took a sip of coffee.

"Only the men were. I've printed out the police reports Houston Metro PD faxed over." Spelling slid a folder to me and one to J.T. "The FBI field office is expecting you and will assist with anything you need. Jade, you and J.T. are heading out now. Review the reports on the plane so you can hit the ground running. You'll check in with SSA Michelle Tam when you get to the field office. She'll update you if anything new came in after these reports." Spelling glanced at the wall clock. "Let's move. Wheels up in forty-five minutes."

J.T. pushed back his chair and stood along with the rest of the team. "You do have a go bag here, right?"

"Yeah, in the ladies' room locker."

"Okay, there should be a car waiting for us out back. I'll meet you there in five." J.T. headed down the hall at a quickened pace.

I stared in disbelief for a second then took off for the ladies' room, almost giddy with anticipation. In the restroom, I used the facilities, grabbed my go bag, and slid the folder containing the Houston police reports into the side pocket. I headed to the exit door and met J.T. in the parking lot. We climbed into the backseat of the waiting black sedan, and the driver pulled out into traffic. We'd be at Mitchell International Airport in under a half hour.

"How can we get through the airport that quickly?" I asked as I situated myself and fastened my seat belt.

"We can't. We're going to a private hangar. The government actually has a large fleet of vehicles and airplanes for federal employees to use. There's always one or two jets available for the serial crimes unit, and as taxpayers, we're paying for that convenience, anyway."

"Wow, I had no idea." I grinned from ear to ear.

Twenty minutes later, we climbed the steps of the fourteen-passenger Gulfstream and within minutes were taxiing out to the runway.

"Let's sit over here," J.T. said and pointed at two comfortable looking chairs with a glossy wooden table situated between them.

I slid the go bag under my seat and fastened the seat belt.

"Make sure your electronics are powered down temporarily. We can roam around the aircraft once we reach cruising altitude. I'll make coffee, then we'll go over the case. There's usually snacks stashed on board too."

"That sounds great. Do I have time to type out a quick text to my sister?"

"Sure, you still have about five minutes. The pilot will let us know when we need to switch over to airplane mode."

I watched as J.T. focused on his phone too. He was probably letting his sister know he wouldn't be home for dinner, just as I was.

"Never married?"

J.T. glanced up from his phone. "Are you talking to me?"

I laughed then looked around the cabin. "I don't see anyone here except you and me. The pilot can't hear us."

"That's one thing I like about you, Jade, you don't mince words."

"No need to. So?"

"Nah, never found the right gal. But then I'd have to be looking, right? I guess I'm just comfortable with the status quo."

"That's understandable."

"And you?"

"I was married for five minutes." I chuckled. "Actually, I was married to someone I thought would be my one and only husband."

"Then what happened?"

"Then he replaced me."

"Ouch!"

"That was a couple of years ago, and I'm over it. I really do enjoy sharing my house with my little sister, Amber."

"The one who wants to be a profiler?"

"Yeah, she's a force, that's for sure, and my only sibling. She has a cat, Spaz, and I have two lovebirds, Polly and Porky." I grinned when I realized J.T. seemed to be enjoying our conversation.

Ten minutes later, at thirty thousand feet, a coffee in front of me, and my folder opened on the table, I looked out the window at the fluffy clouds to my left and the vast landscape beneath me.

"What's on your mind, Jade?" J.T. asked.

"I don't know. I guess nothing in particular."

He looked at me thoughtfully. "We're good at rooting out lies. Spotting a lie comes second nature to us and was part of our training. Yours too, I imagine."

I shrugged and let out a sigh. "It's peaceful up here, looking out."

"It is. And?"

"And I had a memory, that's all. It'll pass."

"Is it too personal to share? We're partners, you know. You may as well spill the beans so I have a chance to plead my case to Spelling. He can reassign you to someone else."

I grinned. "I'm happy with an unencumbered partner, thanks." I paused briefly. "It's a memory of my dad. I pictured him looking out a window like this. He always enjoyed flying, and he'd peer out the windows for hours and take in the beautiful sunrays and cloud formations. He'd always mention how much he loved flying over the Rockies. Over time, he even got good at recognizing the different ski resorts. He loved the Midwest farm country too. He said the fields always reminded him of patchwork quilts."

J.T.'s eyes twinkled as he nodded. "Memories of Tom Monroe have to be good ones."

His words surprised me. "How did you know?"

"I'm a news junkie. I read a lot. Actually, I followed everything the press put out about your dad's murder and how Max Sims is still at large. You guys sure tried hard with all the press coverage, yet he was never apprehended."

"I'll find him in time."

"I'm sorry for your loss, Jade. If you ever feel like talking—"

"Thanks. Maybe we should go over these files."

"Sure, no problem." He opened his folder and began reading the police reports.

I appreciated J.T.'s offer, but I didn't know the man well enough to share my heart and soul with him. He wasn't Jack or the lieutenant, or even Billings and Clayton, and he didn't know my dad. That part of my life and those raw feelings would stay close to my heart for now.

J.T. summarized the reports out loud again. "So two of the three murders involved a missing body part and a bloody cinder block. The reports say the guy whose hands were chopped up worked at a cement company. We definitely need to find out if there's any connection to his job."

I wrote that down. "According to the forensics lab at the PD, no prints have come up at any of the crime scenes. Something rough and porous like a cement block is nearly impossible to pull prints off of, but even with the guy in the tub, they said there weren't any unidentified prints."

"I've been told the same about porous surfaces, although I've never been involved in a scenario where we had to try to get them."

"The killer would be someone strong too, right?"

J.T. nodded. "I'd say so, but the crime scenes should tell us more. We can't rule out an accomplice, either. Even though we have the reports, we have to go over everything again ourselves, and we need to see every photograph the forensic team has too."

"True enough. I had a strange case nearly a year ago that involved a psychic. She was the targeted victim, so we brought her in on the case after she pleaded for us to take her seriously."

J.T. smirked. "Really?"

"Hold that smirk, mister. That's exactly what I did for two years while she begged for someone to believe in her."

"So what happened?"

"There was a man that swore he'd kill her as soon as he got out of prison. She began dreaming about murders once he was released. She kept detailed notes of her dreams down to the tiniest detail. In hindsight, everything she saw in her dreams was scary accurate."

"What was the outcome?"

"The bad guy was real and came after her, so I killed him."

"I think I read about that in the paper. That was you?"

"Uh-huh."

J.T. turned his head and stared out the window. "I'll be damned."

Chapter 7

We landed at George Bush Intercontinental Airport without incident. I watched out the window as the jet came to a stop and the pressurized door was released. We gathered our belongings and exited the jet down the seven steps built into the door. A black extended van waited on the tarmac to whisk us off to the Houston field office.

I was told the drive would take a half hour. We sat quietly and made small talk with the driver about the comfortable Texas weather.

I noted the street signs as we turned off of Federal Plaza Drive, onto Retton Drive, and around the final curve that turned into Justice Park Drive. I knew we had to be close. As we rounded the curve, I saw one large building that definitely stood out among the other few. The building looked to have seven or eight stories and stood alone within a well-manicured lawn surrounded by young trees. The entire perimeter was wrapped with wrought-iron fencing. Our van approached the guard shack nestled between a large gate for entering and another for exiting.

"Pull out your credentials, Jade. The guard needs to see all of them."

"Okay, here you go."

J.T. passed our badges to the driver, who handed them to the guard. The guard stuck his head in the driver's window, looked at our faces to make sure they matched the image on the badge, told us to have a nice day, and handed our badges back to the driver. He returned to the guard shack and pressed the button that released the gate.

The van pulled up to the main entrance, and the driver got out. He came around the van, released the sliding side door, and helped us out. A large covered entrance lay ahead of us, and the double doors to the main lobby wore the FBI logo.

I chuckled. "Apparently this is the right place."

J.T. smiled and pulled the handle on the glass door. The reception area was brightly lit with floor-to-ceiling windows, and a beautiful atrium filled a good area to my right. We approached a large marble counter and showed our credentials then asked where we'd find SSA Michelle Tam.

"Agent Tam is on the fourth floor, office number sixteen. You can leave your bags behind the counter for now."

J.T. nodded and thanked the receptionist. "Looks like the elevators are this way," he said as he pointed to our right.

We followed the wide hallway to a bank of six elevators that lined two walls. J.T. hit the button for the up elevator. I remained quiet. If I let on how impressed I was, I'd appear to be nothing more than a small-town country girl. I stared at the floor and smiled inside. We waited as people exited the elevator, then we boarded. I pressed the button for the fourth floor, and we rode up in silence. Once the doors opened, we walked the long corridor to office sixteen and entered. A receptionist greeted us, and we signed in. She asked us to take a seat and picked up the phone. I assumed she was calling SSA Tam.

Within minutes, a nice looking woman, likely in her early forties, came through a side door and into the reception area where we waited. Her glossy black hair was pulled back in a classic knot, and she was dressed in business casual attire. She greeted us with a warm handshake and introduced herself as Michelle Tam.

"Please, follow me," she said as we passed through a set of doors that took us to a conference room.

We sat with our folders on the table in front of us. Several on-site agents joined us and introduced themselves as Dave Miller and Bruce Starks. They were the go-to agents for any help we needed during our stay. A pitcher of water and a tray of glasses sat on the table. I poured myself a glass and passed the pitcher around.

Michelle Tam began by telling us that formalities weren't necessary. She joked by saying her title was far too long to be used every time someone addressed her. Calling her by Agent Tam, or boss, was fine.

She cleared her throat and began. "The information you have is what local law enforcement gave us. As of this morning, nothing has changed. Three murders in the last week in the metro Houston area isn't something that's completely unheard of, but the methodology and the likely murder weapon, cement in one form or another, connects them. There's also the mutilation that concerns me. All of the similarities combined led the police department to believe a serial killer may be roaming the streets of Houston. Early this morning, Beverly Grant was located with a cement block next to her head, and her tongue had been removed. Her mutilation, along with the block, was enough for the police department to consider her a third victim. We haven't had any alerts since. If you notice in the police reports, the victims don't seem to be targeted by race, age, religion, or gender, so I'd rule out a hate crime in its normal sense." Agent Tam paused to take a sip of water.

"Ma'am, may I?" I said.

"Certainly, Agent Monroe, you have the floor."

I stood and began. "I've had a personal experience similar to this one in the past, and in a sense, it actually is a hate crime. The hate is in the eyes of the killer, and they aren't targeting a particular race, religion, or gender. Since the victims don't have a personal connection, as in a work relationship, the same friends, or family in common, the only connection would have to come from the killer's point of view. There's something these people did that wronged him or her." I paused while several people took notes, then continued. "Upon the coroner's initial exam at each scene, he reported two evenly spaced burn marks on everyone's neck, indicative of a stun gun. This is likely how the unsub disorients the victims before the actual murder takes place. That's telling me the killer could either be a small person that needs an edge to subdue the victim or they have an accomplice that distracts the victim while the other hits them with the gun. A blitz attack, so to speak."

"Good point, Agent Monroe. Go ahead."

"Thank you, ma'am. Think of road rage as an example. There's a trigger that sets off the perp. He or she may run a totally unsuspecting driver off the road, they may shoot someone that's sitting at a red light, or even follow a person to their workplace or home. None of these victims have anything in common with each other, but to the offender, they need to pay because somehow he or she was wronged. The trigger could be something as simple as a driver switching lanes suddenly, turning without using their directional, or even brake checking because the perp rode their bumper."

"That's right, and all of those scenarios have actually happened numerous times throughout the last ten years or so," J.T. added.

"Great point, both of you. Let's put the connection between the victims on the back burner for now and get in the head of the killer. They're obviously trying to convey a message." Agent Tam addressed J.T. and me. "Agents Monroe and Harper, I'd like you to follow up with the people the police interviewed. Dave and Bruce can help out with that."

"Ma'am, we'd also like to go out to the crime scenes ourselves. There may be critical information remaining that could give us important clues."

"Absolutely, Agent Monroe, and there are cars in the lot available for your use. Ask at the reception counter downstairs. Let's meet back at"—she checked the time— "five o'clock, here in the conference room, and see what we have. That's it for now."

Back downstairs, Dave and Bruce sat with J.T. and me around a table near the building's entrance as we divided up the names by location. That was the most logical way to approach the follow-up interviews so we wouldn't spend the day driving all over Houston. We began narrowing down people by phone calls to make sure we knew their whereabouts and whether they were available. That gave us a good number of people that day to speak with face to face. The 9-1-1 operator, Beverly Grant, lived on the outskirts of Houston to the east. Agents Miller and Starks pursued that one together so they could talk to the husband, who worked from home, the neighbors, and the occasional babysitter. They were located within a three-mile radius of each other. J.T. went to speak with the owner of Cornerview Surveying, the company Ted Arneson worked for, and then to the man's home to talk to the wife. The bricklayer, the second person killed, worked for a large company on the outskirts of Houston called Cemcom. I'd take that one.

We walked together to the parking lot, where we were told to look for vehicles that had a red sticker on the windshield. Those were the government-issued vehicles that were at our disposal for the time we were there. Agent Tam suggested we check into our rooms, freshen up, then hit the road within the hour. J.T. and I parted ways with Agents Miller and Starks and drove to the Lone Star Suites, only a mile up the road, where two rooms had been reserved in our names.

We checked in and rode the elevator to the third floor. "Looks like our rooms are across the hall from each other," I said as I slipped the key card into the slot and pushed the door open to room 302.

J.T. did the same for room 305. "Hungry?"

"A little. We did miss lunch unless you call a granola bar and coffee on the jet 'lunch.'"

"How long is it going to take you to freshen up?"

I laughed. "I don't know, I've never timed myself. Ten minutes, maybe."

"Good. I'll bang on your door in ten minutes. We'll grab something at that fast-food restaurant we passed on the way over here then split up after we eat."

"Sure, sounds good. I better get at that freshening-up thing. The clock is ticking."

A half hour later, we were sitting at an outdoor table, wolfing down our burgers and fries.

"I'll admit, brushing my teeth and washing my face does make me feel better. How far is that surveyor's place of employment?"

J.T. punched a few keys on his phone. "Twenty minutes from here. That's doable. And Cemcom?"

"A little farther. I believe it's forty minutes away. Why are we interviewing the same people the police already have?"

He swiped the air with a French fry. "It happens all the time. We need our own reports to go off of too since we'll probably ask different questions than they did. That way we can combine our information with the police reports, do a lot of brainstorming, and come up with more leads. The more data we have to work with, the sooner we catch this wacko."

"I guess the procedure isn't much different no matter what branch of law enforcement you're in." I coated a fry with ketchup and bit into it. "I think I'm going to like being an FBI agent. We aren't confined to county and state borders, and we can really use our skills to pursue the worst offenders."

"That's what it's about, Jade, getting the bad guys off the street."

J.T. stared at me a little longer than I felt comfortable with. I knew he was reading my thoughts.

"Don't worry, we'll get him. Max Sims is far from brilliant. He'll slip up sooner or later."

"I'd prefer sooner." I wiped my mouth, balled up the wrappers, and tossed them in the nearest trash can. A brisk wind swept across the outdoor patio area. I looked up at the sky. "It looks like the weather is changing. Shall we?"

Chapter 8

The increasing wind whipped across the freeway and the memories returned of the storm on the last night of my dad's life.

Knock it off and focus on the GPS directions and your driving. You need both hands on the wheel with these wind gusts.

I wasn't accustomed to being in a sea of traffic, let alone freeways that were five lanes on each side. The drive needed my full attention, especially when I wasn't familiar with where I was going. The robot voice on my phone said I was to exit the freeway a half mile up. I clicked my blinker to move over three lanes to my right. That in itself was a challenge. I wasn't used to big cities, and Houston was nearly four times the size of Milwaukee.

I took in a deep breath and relaxed my tight shoulders when I made it to the far right lane and exited the freeway. I turned right at the lights. I needed to go up three blocks to the intersection of Forty-Third and Franklin and turn left on Franklin. Franklin would take me out of Houston, and Cemcom was supposed to be at the end of the road. I drove at least five miles before I saw a monolith of a complex straight ahead. Enormous stacks and silos at the end of that dead-end road—along with multiple buildings all covered with a fine gray silt—told me I was at the right place. A sign at the fence had Cemcom written across it. I followed the road in and parked alongside the dust-covered cars, thankful that the wind was coming from the other side of the buildings. Wearing cement dust all afternoon wasn't part of my fashion plan.

I shielded my eyes as I walked at a quickened pace toward what looked to be the entrance of the complex. A long sidewalk, shaded by a pergola, led visitors and office employees to a grand foyer with a stained and polished cement floor. It was actually quite beautiful, and there was no shortage of cement at this facility, anyway. I walked up to a reception counter and asked the first woman that acknowledged me to direct me to the person that was bricklayer Jerry Fosco's foreman.

Her name tag read "Agnes," and she stared at me as if I were crazy. "Ma'am, Cemcom employs four thousand individuals that are constantly on shift rotations. We have workers on the twelve-hour shifts, around the clock, and also the three eight-hour shifts, around the clock, as well. I need to know the shift Jerry worked and the day in question. This company never shuts down production."

I didn't appreciate her tone and tried to make my point as I leaned forward across the counter with the cockiest grin I could muster. "Would you mind telling me how many of those four thousand employees lay brick at night, in the dark? I imagine that could eliminate half of them right out of the gate."

She was dumbstruck and without a smart comeback. "It's going to take a few minutes. Have a seat"—she pointed—"over there."

I pulled out my badge. "Try to put a rush on that."

I grabbed a magazine out of the rack and walked to a grouping of comfortable looking upholstered chairs. I plopped down and flipped pages. I was surprised to see the same woman approach me just minutes later.

"I can lead you to the department you need. Ask for Bob Giles."

"Wonderful." I pulled out my notepad and wrote that name down as I followed her up a flight of stairs.

She opened a door that had "Payroll" written across it.

"Are you sure this is where we want to be?"

"It's the fastest way to track Jerry Fosco's most recent foreman. The bricklayers are in a different division than the people that make the cement. Payroll has his name and the department head he worked for. Bob Giles is in charge of payroll. Tell him the name. He'll track down Jerry's boss." She walked away.

I shook my head with confusion. I'd have thought that in this day and age, a few phone calls could have put me in touch with the proper person. I was sure Agnes had just long hauled me as payback for my earlier comment. I turned around, but she was gone.

"May I help you?"

I faced the counter to see a pleasant looking young man smiling at me.

"Yes, I need to speak to Bob Giles."

"Sure, give me one second." He picked up the phone and paged Bob Giles to the reception counter. "He should be out any second."

"Thanks."

Bob showed up several minutes later, and I introduced myself. I explained how I needed to speak to the foreman Jerry Fosco had worked for during the last week. What I'd read on the police report showed they spoke only to someone in the personnel department. I wanted to speak to someone that worked directly with the man.

"Sure, come on back. I'll pull that information up for you on my computer."

We entered a small office with one guest chair. Bob motioned for me to sit, and I did. After a few keystrokes, he had the information I needed.

"It looks like Jerry worked the eight-hour day shift last week, and Leroy Haines was in charge. Our method may seem complicated to you, but depending on the shift the employee works and whether it's a day or night shift, the pay is different. We have to keep proper records of that."

"So you're saying I need to speak to Leroy Haines?"

"Yep, he's your man."

"Where can I find him?"

"Well"—Bob scratched his head—"that might be tough."

"Humor me. I like tough."

"He's at a jobsite until four o'clock. Everyone heads back

in after that, cleans up, and punches out for the day."

"How far away is that jobsite? It's imperative that I speak with him today."

"Let's see if I can track down the location." After Bob made a few more keystrokes while I drummed my fingers on my right knee, he had the location. "You're in luck. It's only three miles from here. Would you like the address?"

"I'd love the address."

Chapter 9

Jordan heard the door between the garage and kitchen open and close. She glanced at the wall clock and wondered why Kent was back home. The notepad she had sitting on her lap was quickly slipped under the recliner's cushion for now. There was nothing she could do about the cigarette smell or the obvious ashtray. She hadn't expected him back until sometime Sunday. Now, he was going to ruin her plans for later. Jordan fumed as she pulled the lever on the side of the recliner and got up. Her anger was palpable when she approached him as he walked into the kitchen from the garage.

"What are you doing back home?"

Kent sneered. "Nice greeting, Jordan. I've only been gone a few hours, and you're sick of me already. Weren't you supposed to have a doctor's appointment this afternoon?"

"No, you must have your dates wrong. Why are you back home?"

"Haven't you been outside? The wind is picking up, and a tropical storm is heading into the gulf. It's supposed to dissipate later tonight, but the farther east I drove, the worse it got. I'm not driving all the way to Louisiana until it's over."

Jordan twisted the wand on the kitchen blinds. She peered out at the sky. "It's windy. So what?"

"Well, you aren't the one that would be driving in it for hours. The wind gusts are already at forty miles an hour. I'll probably leave later tonight and stop at a motel along the way."

"Fine, but for now can you make your sales calls downstairs? I'd hate to interrupt you with my daily activities when you need to concentrate."

"I don't need to make any calls, but it's always nice to feel wanted. Smoking again? Jesus, it stinks in here." Kent went to the window and turned the crank then reached across the counter and pulled the whiskey bottle closer. The cabinet above the sink held the rocks glasses, and he reached in for one. His eye caught a glimpse of the bottles of mood stabilizers and antidepressants that had been pushed to the back of the cabinet. "Trying to hide your meds now too?"

"What are you doing?" Jordan rushed him, but he turned his back to her.

With a quick twist of the bottle cap, he shook out the mood stabilizers into his open palm and counted them. "You haven't taken any of these."

"Give me those damn pills." Jordan pulled his hand back, and the pills dropped to the floor, scattering everywhere.

"I'm calling Dr. Phelps. You haven't taken a single pill. No wonder you behave like a lunatic."

"And that's the opinion of a drunk?"

"Either you take the pills or I make the call. I'll have you committed myself. What's it going to be?"

"Fine, give me the pills. If anyone should be committed, it's you. You're pathetic."

Kent went for his phone. "I'm done."

"No. I'll take the pills." Jordan crawled on the kitchen floor until she found the fifteen pills and put them back in the bottle.

She heard the water running at the sink, where Kent filled a glass.

"Give me the bottle," he said.

She handed it to him. He opened it and counted the pills then kept one out. "Here, take it."

She slipped it into her mouth and wedged it between her teeth and gums.

"Drink the water."

She did.

"Open your mouth so I can see."

She complied then sneered at him. "Satisfied? What do you intend to do on the days you're out of town?"

"I don't know yet." Kent turned his back to her and opened the whiskey bottle. He tipped it over the glass and poured. "I'm hungry. How about a late lunch?" he asked as he took a seat on the recliner.

She spat the pill into the sink and washed it down the drain. "Make it yourself."

Chapter 10

I had to be at the right place. A sign on a construction fence read "Future home of CMS Realtors." Work trucks lined the curb, and more were parked inside the chain-link fence. Most vehicles wore car door magnets that read Cemcom. It appeared that a dozen or so workers were laying the cinder block foundation on this new project.

Walking inside an active construction zone was probably prohibited, but I didn't have a choice. I needed to speak with Leroy Haines. I pushed through the wind that battered my face with gritty sand and headed into the construction area, but I was stopped before I got my dust-covered right shoe beyond the fence.

"Hey, lady, nobody is allowed back here without a hard hat and proper footwear."

I tried to pinpoint the person who yelled that out, but I couldn't tell one face from another through the brown haze. I cupped my hands around my mouth and yelled back. "I need to speak with Leroy Haines right away."

A man nodded, pulled off his hard hat, and wiped his

brow. He called out to his crew to wrap things up for the day since the dusty wind impeded their work. He walked toward me with a disgruntled expression on his face. I held out my badge so we could cut to the chase.

"Mr. Haines?"

"Yep, that's me." He leaned in and studied my badge. "An FBI agent? Now what did I do?" He smirked and pointed at a small construction trailer. "Come on inside. Let's get out of this wind so we can talk."

The interior of the trailer was about what I expected, but at least we were somewhere quiet. I sucked it up and sat on a grime-covered chair. I wasn't sure if the dark pants I wore helped or not.

"Mr. Haines, I'd like to ask you a few questions about Jerry Fosco. I understand he worked under your supervision for at least the last week. Am I correct?"

"Yeah, Jerry worked for me. Sorry to hear about his demise, but I'm not surprised."

"Really? Can you expand on that for me?" I opened the folder and pulled out my notepad and pen.

"Yeah, he had a short fuse. He didn't work for me often, maybe one week out of every two months, but he always seemed to alienate the other bricklayers. Nobody worked as hard as he did, nobody did as good of a job as he did… it went on and on. He riled up a lot of people, I'll tell you that. I even wrote him up a few times for his conduct."

I opened the folder and read the short paragraph that came from the personnel office.

"They didn't mention Jerry getting written up in their

statement to the police department."

"Yeah, my bad. I told him I'd turn the slips in if he acted up one more time. They're still sitting in my desk drawer."

"Is there any one person in particular that stands out?"

"Nah, he fought with everyone. It was just his nature. The shifts changed so often that the same people hardly ever worked together. Jerry was someone that spouted off too much, but I can't picture anyone doing him in over comments at work." Leroy shook his head. "Nope, I can't think of one person that would do anything like murder. What actually happened?"

I smiled. "Nice try, but you know I can't share the details with anyone outside law enforcement. It's an ongoing investigation, but I'd like to show you a picture of a cinder block."

"Cinder block?" He chuckled. "I know what a cinder block looks like, ma'am."

The information about the common murder weapon found at each scene had never been shared with the press. The police department wasn't quite yet prepared to let the public know there was a possible serial killer roaming the streets of Houston.

"Please humor me." I pulled out the photograph of the cinder block found at Jerry's murder scene. I was thankful there was more than one picture of it. I showed Leroy a side view photo that didn't have blood evidence on it. "Is there any way to identify those blocks by the company that makes them? I've heard there are a number of cement factories in the greater Houston area."

"I can't speak for other companies, but our molds are specific to Cemcom and to the type of job we're doing. We have decorative block, functional block, and a hybrid of both."

I handed Leroy the photo, and he studied it closely.

"This is a functional cinder block with a decorative façade. In other words, a hybrid. We use them primarily for residential retaining walls."

"Is this one of yours?"

"Yep, it sure is. Our interior cutouts are a bit unique. The large opening that is filled with cement is actually shaped like two *c*'s facing each other. It's supposed to represent Cemcom, which is an acronym of the words 'cement company.'"

"That's very interesting information, Leroy. Thank you. May I have a contact number in case I need to follow up with you about Jerry?"

"Oh sure, here you go." Leroy pulled a card out of his shirt pocket and handed it to me.

"May I have one more so I can write my contact information on the back for you? I don't have my cards with me." That was a white lie, but Leroy didn't need to know my business cards hadn't arrived yet. I thanked him and left then headed back to the field office. I called J.T. as I drove. "How was your meet and greet?" I asked when he answered.

"I just left the surveyor's home. Poor lady. The bathroom was being remodeled since the tub was ruined."

"Not to mention her husband's life."

"Yeah, no shit. Anyway, the wife said he didn't have any enemies, was loved by neighbors and every family member, and they had a strong marriage."

I laughed. "Everyone says that until the truth comes out."

"Cynical?"

"You betcha."

J.T. smirked. "Let's discuss that sometime. Anyway, she also said he didn't have a falling out at work with anyone. Apparently, Cornerview Surveying is a small company with only five employees, and they're the best of friends. They all get together for poker every Friday night."

"So, that sounds like a dead end. Each employee was interviewed by the police?"

"Yeah, they all gave formal statements, and so did the wife. I didn't find out anything new from her, either. The statement she gave me was almost verbatim to the police report about being in Orlando at the time. The police checked with the grandparents, and they back up her story."

"Okay, I'm heading in. I should be at the field office in fifteen minutes."

"Yep, see you in a bit."

I glanced at the clock on the dashboard then remembered Texas was the same time zone as Wisconsin. Amber would still be on duty. I'd try her later after I was back in my hotel room.

We gathered in the conference room after everyone had returned to the field office. Michelle Tam stood at the head of the table.

"Okay, what have we got? Hopefully, you've gleaned more information beyond what the police reports show."

Agents Miller and Starks read their reports aloud. They reiterated how nothing seemed terribly different than the existing police reports on the table in front of us.

"Here's the gist of it, Agent Tam," Dave said. "Beverly Grant left work on Wednesday at the same time her coworkers did, mentioned how she had to hurry home, round up the kids, and take them to their karate class. When she never showed up at home and didn't answer her cell phone, the husband went out to look for her. That's when he saw her empty Buick parked along the road. The police didn't discover her mutilated body until this morning after daybreak. The neighbors all said she was cordial enough but spent most of her time with the kids and their after-school activities. None of them knew her as a close friend."

Tam's eyebrows rose in a questioning frown. "No hanky-panky in the marriage?"

"Not according to the husband. Their life insurance policies haven't been updated in ten years, and no unusual bank transactions have taken place," Agent Miller said.

Agent Tam turned to J.T. "Agent Harper, anything new on Ted Arneson?"

"Only that the guys from Cornerview Surveying got together every Friday night for poker. It sounds like they were good friends, and the company only employs five guys."

"That sounds like a dead end, excuse the pun. Agent Monroe?"

"I did find out a bit more than what was noted in the police report. According to a foreman that Jerry Fosco worked directly under, he was a hothead that fought a lot with his coworkers. The foreman, Leroy Haines, didn't think anyone took Jerry's verbal assaults seriously enough to physically harm him. There was one thing I found very helpful, though."

Agent Tam smoothed her hair then gave me a nod.

"Mr. Haines said the cinder block in the police photo was one of theirs, and it was the type most commonly used for residential retaining walls. The only problem with that is those blocks are for sale in every big-box home improvement store across the country. Anyone could have bought them, and anyone could have installed them. According to the Internet, there are forty-two home improvement stores in the greater Houston area that sell cinder blocks."

I saw Agent Tam's shoulders deflate. "So we're back to square one. Okay, call it a day. Everyone be back in this room at eight a.m. I want all the crime scenes revisited tomorrow, and then we'll put together an initial profile with the information we have."

J.T. walked alongside me as we left the field office. "Nice job taking charge earlier. You're going to fit in well, Jade."

"Thanks, I guess it comes naturally once I get over my shyness."

He laughed. "I haven't seen a shy side of your personality yet. Want to ride together to the hotel?"

"Sure, that sounds good."

"How about dinner? Food is part of our stipend, you know."

I noticed his eyes twinkling playfully. He liked to joke, and I was glad of it—it reminded me of Jack. There was a lot about J.T. that reminded me of Jack. Although their hair color and style was different, the good looks, dimples, and sweet disposition were pluses in my opinion. I hoped someday that I would be as close to J.T. as I was to my former partner.

We boarded the elevator together and exited at the third floor. My room was two doors up the hallway on the left.

"How about the restaurant downstairs? I like easy."

I chuckled. "I like easy too. Say in an hour? I want to shower and get out of these dusty clothes."

"Sure. I'll be the one banging on your door at seven o'clock."

Chapter 11

Kent was three sheets to the wind by the time dinner was prepared and the table had been set. Each place setting contained a charger under the plate, a napkin next to the fork on the left, the knife blade faced inward on the right, and the spoon sat beside the knife. The water glass was at the one o'clock position above the plate. A bowl of roasted peppers and mushrooms sat next to a platter of almond-crusted cod in the center of the table. Despite Kent's insistence that she needed mood stabilizers and antidepressants, Jordan knew that she was actually extremely focused and an accomplished cook.

She tapped Kent's shoulder then picked up the television remote to turn off the local evening news. Just as her thumb touched the red Off button, Jordan paused and stared at the screen. The segment focused on several murders that had taken place over the last week. At the time of the broadcast, even though the FBI had been called in to assist local law enforcement, nobody was in custody. Jordan gave that some thought—she had more people to deal with and not a lot of time to accomplish the task. The fact that Kent was home had already put her behind schedule.

Even more irritated, she pushed Kent's shoulder harder. "Wake up if you intend to eat supper." She mumbled under her breath, "Pathetic drunk."

"What? What do you want?"

"Get up. Dinner is on the table."

Kent pulled himself to his feet. "I've got to wash up first." He held the walls as he stumbled to the bathroom.

Jordan pulled the legal pad out from under the recliner cushion and took it into the bedroom. She slipped it under the mattress on her side of the bed. Once Kent left, she would continue outlining her plan of attack for the next name on the list.

Chapter 12

"Of course it's different. The traveling will take some getting used to, but it's what I want and need to do."

"And what are the agents in Houston like?"

I rearranged myself on the chair and took a guilt-free break before dinner to call Amber. My hair had to dry, anyway, and J.T. wouldn't be banging on my door for another thirty-five minutes.

"They seem nice enough, and I'm getting to know J.T. better every day."

Amber giggled wickedly into the phone.

"Don't even start with me. Look how long Jack and I were partners. There's nothing now, or ever, that's going to happen beyond a work relationship."

"When am I going to meet him?"

"Who knows. It isn't like I'm going to host a backyard barbecue this time of year."

"We could host an indoor Sunday football game party."

"Maybe, I'll have to give that some thought. I don't know if that's considered fraternizing or not. I will admit,

though, J.T. is as good looking as Jack, and he's really nice."
While Amber talked, I sipped the glass of water I had
poured from the complimentary bottle next to the
microwave.

"J.T. Harper? That sounds like a name in a made-for-
TV cop show."

"No kidding, right? Anyway, I've got to get ready for
dinner. How's everything at home and work?"

"It's all good, and I feel safe with the alarm system.
Thanks, sis."

"You got it, hon. I'll talk to you tomorrow. Tell the boys
hi for me, and give Polly and Porky a big kiss."

"Will do."

I clicked off and went back into the bathroom to dry my
hair and fix my makeup. I had twenty minutes to get ready.
As soon as I had on a clean pair of pants and a lightweight
sweater, a bang sounded on the door. I laughed, wiped my
dusty shoes on the bath mat, and opened the door.

J.T. looked surprised. "Humph."

"What does *that* mean?" I asked as I tucked my door key
into my pants pocket and grabbed my purse and phone.

"I have two sisters, that's what *humph* means. I've never
known a woman that was ready to go anywhere on time."

I shut the door at my back. "Until now."

Downstairs at the lobby restaurant and bar, we browsed
the menu as the waitress took our drink order.

"What is our travel food stipend?" I asked when I
noticed the expensive fare.

"Fifty dollars a day. Not bad considering we've only had

a hamburger and fries today on the FBI's tab. Order whatever you want. What you have left will easily cover the prices on the menu."

"The FBI is crazy different than the sheriff's department. We didn't have stipends."

"You were also a county employee, not a federal employee."

"True. I think I'm having the sirloin tips over noodles and a tossed salad."

"Nice choice. I'm having the skirt steak and a baked potato with carrots."

The waitress brought our drinks and took our dinner order.

"So you're a Scottish Ale enthusiast?"

"Absolutely. Nothing finer, and apparently you like the local craft beers." I sipped the foam, my favorite part, then set the beer glass down. I propped my chin in my hands on the table and stared across at J.T. "What's your gut telling you about this killer?"

"They're somebody that plans things out well in advance. That means they have time on their hands. They either work from home, don't work at all, or can somehow plan their schedule around the victim they're targeting. All three victims were ambushed in the evening, meaning the killer knew their route home and where they lived."

I leaned in and took a deep gulp of my ale. "The person must be strong enough to not care about the volume of cement it took to fill a tub or the weight of those heavy cinder blocks. I mean why carry that stuff around? Use a hammer or something lighter, for Pete's sake."

J.T. chuckled. "I don't believe you just said that."

"Well, seriously. Cement has to represent something. There's no other reason to use it."

"That's a fact. Let's see how our combined information shapes up in the morning."

J.T. and I talked about the case over dinner. By nine thirty, I was back in my room and relaxing on the bed in my pajamas. With the TV on and the volume low, I listed my own ideas of what the killer's motivation might be. I checked the time again before I clicked off the light. I figured Jack would still be awake, and I missed my old partner. I made the call, and we touched base for fifteen minutes. I hung up with a smile on my face and closed my tired eyes.

Chapter 13

He was definitely trying her patience. Kent needed four cups of coffee to wake himself up enough to leave for the second time that day. Jordan stared at the clock and paced as he rearranged his suitcase and dropped his toothbrush and toothpaste into his bathroom travel kit.

Finally, at eleven o'clock, he gave her a peck on the cheek, grabbed his bag, and exited the house through the door that led to the garage. Jordan heard the overhead lift and Kent's car start. With her fingertips, she pulled the sheers aside on the sidelights at the front door and watched him back down the driveway. Within seconds, his brake lights flashed at the end of the block, then he disappeared around the corner.

She grumbled when he was finally out of sight. "It's about damn time you left." She set her cell phone alarm for three a.m., reviewed her notes one last time, and went to bed.

The chirping alarm woke her from that deep sleep. The bed was warm and comfortable—she enjoyed sleeping alone. Kent disgusted her, and having him lie in bed so close was nearly intolerable, but she'd deal with him later.

Jordan threw the blankets to the side and climbed out. The dark attire she had placed on the side chair lay neatly folded and ready to slip on. With everything she needed already placed in the backpack, she exited the house and headed to Store-All to pick up the van. She glanced at the time as she drove. Jordan needed to be inside murder number four's house in fifty minutes and not a second later. She'd planned her route in advance, and she'd enter through the park that ran parallel to the back property lines of the homes on his block. Arriving there before daylight would keep her well-hidden at the back of his house as she entered. With the window ajar in that extra room, entering the home would be a cake walk.

Jordan slowed the van to a stop at the park trail head and exited the vehicle. She'd have a ways to go through the darkened woods before she reached his home. Fifteen minutes into the walk, she stopped to count the number of homes on that street. His was directly ahead. Jordan crouched as she made her way to that back window, quietly lifted the glass, then lowered her backpack to the floor inside. Being tall helped—she easily reached over the sill, pressed her feet on the wall, and heaved herself over the window's ledge.

She knelt on the floor as she gathered the immediate tools she needed. The syringe was already loaded and ready. That and the stun gun were dropped into her right jacket pocket, and a small flashlight filled the left. She removed her shoes and crept out of the room.

His bedroom was the next room on the right, and the door was open just enough that she didn't have to wonder about creaky hinges. Jordan slipped through without making a sound. A quick flick of the flashlight showed her how he was lying in the bed. His neck was exposed enough that the stun gun could do its job. He'd be disabled long enough for her to inject him with the sedative.

She felt the familiar shape in her pocket and pulled it out. Her thumb found the round button that would send excruciating electric volts through his body and render him senseless. Jordan crept closer until she was right above him. She leaned in and nailed him in the neck. He grunted, and his body arched then fell limp. Jordan hit the light switch next to the door. She had only a minute at best. With the protective end cap held between her teeth, she pulled the syringe out, exposed the needle, and pierced his skin. Pressing the plunger until it stopped, Jordan emptied the barrel of Methohexital into his neck. She had an hour to complete her task.

Forty minutes before dawn would lighten the sky, Jordan found the car keys, backed his vehicle out of the garage, parked it in the driveway, and slipped away, apparently unseen. She jogged the several blocks to the van, climbed inside, and drove it to his house. With the van secured out of sight behind the closed overhead garage door, she continued where she'd left off. With one block under each arm, Jordan made three trips to and from the garage to the bedroom. Finally, satisfied with the six cinder blocks that pinned him down, she went to the guest room and retrieved her backpack. Jordan pulled out the vinyl-coated apron, slipped it over her head, and tied it at her back. Things were about to get messy.

His cell phone sat only a foot away on the nightstand, and she grabbed it to check the time—five o'clock. He'd be waking up soon. With everything in place, Jordan made a cup of instant coffee for herself, returned to the bedroom, and waited.

Ten minutes later, he began to stir and gradually woke up. His heavy lids finally opened fully. She could tell by his initial expression of confusion, which quickly turned to terror, that the reality of his predicament was sinking in. His eyes darted across the room until they stopped on her.

"Who the hell are you and why are you in my bedroom?" Fear elevated and tightened his voice.

Mark Fellenz woke to find his arms tied to the headboard and his legs weighed down with cinder blocks. He looked from side to side then down at his legs. His panicked expression amused Jordan. He couldn't move, let alone get to his phone to call for help.

She sat on a chair two feet from Mark's face. A single unused cinder block remained on the floor beside her.

"You don't know me, do you, Mark? I don't look the least bit familiar to you, do I?"

"No, you psycho bitch, so get out of my house." He wrenched at the ropes and tried to loosen them. The headboard rattled against the wall. "How did—" He grimaced in pain. "What the hell is going on? Why do I hurt?"

"We'll get to that in a bit. How did I know where you live, or how did I tie you up? Use your words, Mark."

81

"Both." He sucked in a deep breath as his panic increased.

Jordan leaned back in the chair and picked up the cup of coffee that sat on the night table. The man did a double take.

"Yes, I've gotten comfortable since I've been here. That drug takes a while to wear off." She pushed up her sleeve and looked at her watch. "I've been here nearly two hours."

"You drugged me? With what? Why are you wearing gloves?"

"Don't worry about it. That's the least of your problems. What's your job title, Mark?"

"What? My job title?"

"Did I stutter?" Jordan stood and slapped him across the face, bloodying his lip.

He licked the droplet of blood. "You stupid bitch"—he writhed harder but to no avail—"wait until I get out of these restraints."

"Therein lies the problem, Mark. You'll be dead before you ever get those ropes loose enough to do anything to me. I'll make sure of that." She cocked her head and smiled. "Look at me. Granted, we're about the same size, but don't forget you were drugged. I'd clearly have the advantage. Now, back to my question, and I'm only asking one more time. What's your job title?"

"I mix cement, so I guess that makes me a cement mixer."

"Correct answer, and that also makes you responsible." She yanked the blankets back to reveal the work she had done while he was unconscious.

The sheet under the blanket stuck to him and pulled at his chest hair. He yelled in pain. She pulled it back farther, revealing the dried blood. Mark tipped his head down and looked at his chest. Horror took over his face.

"What did you do? Why is my chest bloody?"

"I thought it made a good palette, but the carving is actually on your stomach. Blood transfer, I guess."

"Carving?" He grimaced again and began to hyperventilate.

"Here, take a look. I found a hand mirror in your bathroom." Jordan held the mirror above Mark's midsection. "I know the words are backward from your view, but it says *murderer*."

"I've never killed anyone in my life!"

"Yes you have, maybe indirectly, but your hands are as bloody as the rest of them. It's time to pay the piper, and that would be me. Nobody is coming to look for you, either, just so you know. I've already texted your employer that you've come down with the flu. You'll be spending the day in bed"—she chuckled—"which actually is true. My question for you is, would you rather die quickly or slowly?"

He stared at her, his eyes clouded with fear. Either answer would ensure his demise. "Slowly?"

"Nah, that's too boring. I like fast and violent. It's time to live in the same hell I do every day."

Jordan reached down and picked up the final cinder block. With a hard and violent thrust, she caved in Mark's forehead. Blood gushed, and his eyes rolled back. She watched him twitch a few times, then his body went limp. Jordan prodded and poked at him, but he didn't move. As a final measure, she removed the hatchet from her backpack, and with a thrust back, then forward, she hacked through both wrists that were tied to the bedposts. Mark's dismembered hands fell to the bed on either side of him.

"There, now your hands truly *are* bloody."

Jordan crossed the room and entered the master bath. Inside, she took off her socks, rolled up her pant legs, and stepped into the shower. She slipped off the vinyl apron, washed it thoroughly with the shower hose, and wrapped that, along with the washed hatchet and gloves, in a plastic bag. She stepped out onto the bath rug, put her socks on, and slipped on a clean pair of gloves. With her shoes back on, she closed the spare bedroom window and left through the garage. She had just enough time to get in the van and make a quiet exit before the neighborhood began buzzing with people leaving for work.

Once home, Jordan put away her supplies and crawled back into bed.

Her ringing cell phone woke her at seven o'clock. Jordan checked the screen—Jeanie was calling.

"Hello."

"Did I wake you? You sound sleepy. I've texted you twice already, but you didn't respond."

"I couldn't sleep last night, so I stayed up and worked on my to-do list. I guess I dozed off again."

"Do you want to go to the mall with me later? I have the shopping bug, then we can stop for lunch afterward."

"I have too much to do today. I need to whittle away at my list. I'm making progress, though. I've crossed the halfway point."

"Do you need help with anything?"

"Hardly. I'll talk to you later."

"It's been a while, Jordan. I miss you. Are you all right?"

"I'm fine. Bye." Jordan hung up and propped the pillows against the headboard. She enjoyed going back to that dark place where she relived each ambush and kill. It made her eager to complete the next job.

Chapter 14

I read the comments and funny anecdotes from Jack and Amber as I rode the elevator down to the banquet room where I was meeting J.T. for a continental breakfast. I chuckled at their early morning humor and tapped off several quick responses. Those two meant the world to me. I had just enough time to check the FBI's Ten Most Wanted list when the elevator stopped at the second floor. With my thumb and index finger, I expanded the screen. The photo of Max Sims's face stared at me. His hollow eyes were filled with hatred. Someday, the words CAPTURED or DECEASED in bright red text would cover his photo. I hoped for the latter, and I wanted to be the person standing over him when he drew his last breath. I pocketed my phone and exited the elevator when the doors parted on the first floor.

"Hey, partner," J.T. said when he saw me enter the banquet room. "How'd you sleep?"

He was so much like Jack that I had to watch myself so I wouldn't accidentally call him by the wrong name.

"I must have slept pretty good considering I don't remember my head hitting the pillow. Now I'm raring to go." I checked the breakfast menu on the chalkboard behind the counter. "I'm having scrambled eggs and bacon. How about you?" I stood and grabbed a tray.

"I'm not much of a breakfast guy. A bagel and coffee is all I need."

"Suit yourself. My sister is the cook at home, and she spoils me rotten. Who does the cooking at your house?"

"Julie, of course, but she has it relatively easy since I'm gone a lot."

"Want a refill?" I held up a coffee mug.

"Yeah, thanks."

I set down my tray and took a seat. "How long do out-of-state cases usually take?"

"There's no normal. Sometimes I'm gone a week, but usually it's a bit less."

"Good to know." I picked up a strip of bacon and popped it into my mouth. "How can you pass this up? Bacon is like manna from heaven."

J.T. laughed.

We were in the conference room by seven fifty, each with a cup of coffee in hand. Dave Miller and Bruce Starks walked in right behind us. We found the same seats we had yesterday, took out our folders and notepads, and waited for Michelle Tam. The sound of heels clacking against the tile hallway told us she was likely the person getting closer to the conference room. Agent Tam entered, gave us a short, to-the-point greeting, and began.

"We have another victim found less than an hour ago. Strangely enough, the MO has changed slightly. This man, Mark Fellenz, was viciously attacked in his home while he was still in bed. According to the county ME, he's been dead for less than two hours. A neighbor leaving for work noticed his car parked in the driveway and the overhead garage door open. According to the neighbor, Mark was naturally cautious and would never forget to close the garage door. After getting no response through phone calls and knocking, the neighbor contacted the police. They opened up the house and discovered his mutilated body."

Dave Miller spoke up. "So it seems the killer is available any time of day or night."

We nodded and jotted down that tidbit.

J.T. asked if there was evidence of stun gun burns on the body or any form of cement at the scene.

Agent Tam sighed. "Yes to both questions. Multiple cinder blocks were found. The victim had stun gun burns on his neck, his hands were dismembered, and the word 'murderer' was etched into his midsection."

"So this *was* a revenge killing. Maybe they all were, but revenge for whom?" I asked.

"That's something we need to work on. The ME and forensic team are on-site, so I want all of you there right now. Leave no stone unturned, people. I want this killer found yesterday. Take a van from the lot and be back here for a follow-up meeting after lunch. The address has been sent to your phones."

We left together, and Dave Miller got behind the wheel

for the twenty-minute drive. Bruce grabbed the passenger seat. J.T. and I sat in the center row and made bullet point notes for the afternoon meeting.

Dave slowed near the police car that blocked Montbark Street. He lowered the window and flashed his badge. The officer peeked in the window, saw all of us wearing FBI-issued windbreakers, and then waved us through. The Houston metro forensic van and coroner's van sat at the curb. Police squad cars blocked through traffic and diverted neighborhood cars onto a different street, and yellow police tape wrapped the perimeter of the yard. Dave parked across the street, and we exited the van. Several officers milled about and checked the shrubbery and detached shed for anything that seemed out of place. I approached one of the officers and extended my hand. He introduced himself as Lee.

"Have your guys found anything outside yet, Lee?"

"No, ma'am, everything appears normal."

"No signs of forced entry?"

"It doesn't appear so."

I raised my brow with concern. "You'll let me know if something seems unusual to you, right?"

"I certainly will, ma'am."

"Thanks." I walked away and jotted that information down in my notepad. I returned to the front of the house, where J.T. waited.

"Where'd you disappear to?" he asked.

"I was making nice with the local boys. It's the easiest way to get information without stepping on toes."

"Good work. Are you ready to go inside?"

"As ready as I'll ever be."

Quarters were cramped inside the two-bedroom, one-bath bungalow. Two officers, the forensic team, and the ME filled the bedroom. There was no chance of getting up close and personal with the victim yet. We turned in the hallway and spread out to other rooms. Nothing in the house appeared disturbed or missing. I peered into the bathroom and noticed an obvious set of footprint indentations in the bath rug. I knelt down and felt the rug with the back of my gloved hand. It was damp. Droplets of water still coated the inside of the tub. I walked out and closed the door behind me.

"Has anyone gone into the bathroom?"

Several officers answered that they had peeked in but hadn't entered. They explained that the forensic team would have to be the ones to go over any potential evidence. Nobody was allowed to disturb the scene.

I smirked. "Yeah, I took Police Protocol 101 too, thanks."

J.T. whispered, "No need to get testy."

I cocked my head. "Come on, seriously? I need to take a picture of that bath rug, though. There are imprints of bare feet. If the ME inks a footprint of the vic for us, we could at least compare the footprint size. The rug is still damp, J.T. We need to keep everyone out of there until forensics is finished in the bedroom. If someone other than the deceased was in the shower, there could be forensic evidence in the tub or sink trap too."

"I'll get someone to keep an eye on the door." J.T.

walked away to get an officer while I continued through the house.

I opened the second bedroom door. The stark space held two mismatched chairs and a row of boxes that lined the right wall. The absence of a bed told me that room wasn't used as a guest room but more of a catchall for unused junk. I pulled out my cell phone. The forensic team was preoccupied, anyway. As long as I looked without touching anything, I was certain I would find something useful waiting to be discovered.

I flipped on the light switch and did an initial left-to-right once-over of the room before I stepped in. I took a picture from the doorway then entered. Nothing lay on the hardwood floor to block my path. My shoes were covered with blue booties, and I walked the room slowly and deliberately. A layer of dust covered the boxes that were propped against the wall. By the way things looked, nobody had touched them for some time. I snapped several pictures and moved on. A singular window across the room caught my eye. The window, devoid of a shade or curtain, was another reminder that the room hadn't been used for anything other than storage. I went to the window and looked out. Beyond the small backyard stood several large boulders standing side by side, leading into the woods.

With a few taps on my phone, I pulled up a satellite view of the address. A park filled several hundred acres of land behind the row of homes on that street. Trails crisscrossed throughout the park and led in dozens of directions. One interesting trail ran parallel to all of the backyards and emptied onto the street a few blocks away. I wrote that in my notepad. I glanced down and thought about this room possibly being the intruder's point of entry. I stared at the sill and realized it was dust free. That fact made no sense unless the window had been recently opened. The distance from the window's base to the ground below was a mere four feet—most anyone could manage that. The missing window screen would have made climbing in a piece of cake. I took a picture of the sill and another through the glass out to the woods. I left the room and closed the door.

I found J.T. checking out the kitchen. "Hey, partner, I'm going to walk the outside perimeter."

"Smell something?"

"Maybe. Want to join me?"

"Sure. The house has been gone over, anyway."

I whispered as we exited the front door, "I hate to say it, but the patrol cops are only here to keep the looky-loos at bay. They aren't thinking like a perp and have no idea what to search for. Come around to the back of the house. I want to check something out."

J.T. followed me around the corner. Several officers searched the shed as we passed by.

"Okay, I want to check near that window." I pointed at the only window other than the patio door that faced the backyard. "Make sure you don't step on anything."

"Meaning?"

"Meaning the perp's footprints. The room beyond the window is a spare bedroom that doesn't get used. Boxes stacked against the wall were covered in dust, yet the windowsill didn't have one speck of dust on it. There isn't a screen covering the window, either. I don't want to touch anything yet, but I bet anybody can push that window up and down with their fingertips."

"So, that could be the point of entry. Something ought to look disturbed if that's the case."

I grinned. "Now you've got the idea. Look at that woods back there." I pointed and scanned left to right. "I pulled up a satellite view earlier. There's a couple-hundred-acre park behind these houses with plenty of trails."

J.T. nodded. "Easy access and nobody would have noticed a thing in the dark."

"You got it, partner."

A low row of bushes was situated beneath the window, making it more difficult for evidence to be noticed—unless one knew what to look for. J.T. and I carefully pushed the shrubbery away from the wall and saw scuff marks under the window.

"I need to take a picture of that," I said to J.T. as he held the shrubs to the side. I clicked off three pictures.

"Those are definitely from shoes. You can faintly make out the tread pattern even though they're just from the instep up to the toes."

I raised my brows in agreement then leaned in closer and clicked off a few more shots. "That's definitely toe pressure from climbing in. That means they grasped the inside of the sill with their fingers to pull themselves through. What do you think the chances are of finding prints?"

J.T. smirked. "I'd say close to zero. The perp was likely

smart enough to be gloved. Check the ground for shoe prints."

We scoured the ground beneath the shrubbery and three feet out beyond the window with no luck. It didn't help that Houston hadn't had a recent rainfall.

I jerked my head toward the house. "Let's tell forensics what we've found in the bathroom, guest room, and out here. They can take over. I want to walk the trail directly behind the houses. According to the satellite imagery, the trail dumps back out onto the street a few blocks away."

After updating forensics on what we'd found, J.T. and I headed into the woods. We walked the trail directly behind the houses, our eyes focused on the ground. With the indigenous trees dropping their leaves this time of year, finding any evidence on the path was nearly impossible. We ended at the street fifteen minutes later with nothing to show for our work but a nice walk in the park. We hadn't found anything unusual on the ground, if that was indeed the route the perp took. We walked back to the house and entered the master bedroom, where Mark Fellenz still lay on the bed.

"Wow, I thought I'd seen everything," J.T. said as he leaned in and stared at the severed hands on the bed. He lifted the sheet and read the word 'murderer' carved on Mark's abdomen.

The scene was bloody, gruesome, and definitely overkill. Reading the police reports from the previous three victims told me those also were horrific scenes, but being up close and personal with this one put an entirely different light on the brutality of the crime.

Dave entered the room. "Have you ever—"

I interrupted him. "Yeah, actually I have, but you never get used to it." I clicked off a few pictures.

Dave smirked. "Now you're moonlighting as a crime lab tech?"

I turned and shot him a frown. "Isn't there something you need to do, Dave? I doubt if Agent Tam sent you along just to critique what I'm doing."

He walked away, and I continued to snap pictures.

J.T. chuckled. "You aren't going to score any points with him."

"Not trying to. I'm actually more interested in doing my job. We aren't going to get anything from forensics today, but Agent Tam wants a report from us. The pictures will help me get into the killer's head." I tucked my cell phone back into my pocket. "Let's see if everyone is ready to head back. It's after lunchtime already."

J.T. checked in with SSA Spelling in Milwaukee and updated him on the case as we made our way back to the Houston field office. Dave pulled into a drive-through restaurant and placed four identical orders. We ate during the drive back.

At one o'clock, we filed into the conference room and took our seats. I flipped through the photos in my phone gallery as we waited for Agent Tam to arrive. The footprint impression on the bath rug and the shoe mark on the outside wall somehow felt off to me.

With my hand cupping the right side of my mouth, I whispered to J.T., "What size shoe do you wear?"

He grinned. "You're a weird one, Monroe, but I wear a size twelve. Why?"

I wrinkled my nose. "Narrow, medium, or wide?"

"Medium, I guess. I don't have to special order shoes. I buy them right off the shelf."

"Don't you think those shoe prints on the wall and the impression on the bath rug look narrower and a bit shorter than a normal-sized man's foot?" I handed J.T. my phone so he could look at the photos again.

"You may have a point. The wall could go either way, but there's an entire print on that rug. I'm sure forensics can do a quick comparison of foot sizes before they get too deep into everything else. What do you think the rug size was, two feet by three feet?"

I thought back. "Yeah, that sounds about right." My mental image was interrupted by the sound of the door opening.

Agent Tam walked in and greeted us for the second time that day. She was tough and didn't beat around the bush, no sugarcoating anything.

"Let's go. Who has something?" She looked from face to face.

Surprisingly, Bruce Starks, the normally quiet one, caught her attention.

"Go ahead, Bruce." Agent Tam took a seat and scooted in her chair.

"Based on the evidence at the scene, my opinion is the killer is a white male, possibly in his mid-thirties. He's strong enough to overpower his victims even though he has used stun guns to help subdue them. He's aggressive and hunts these people like prey. A risk taker. He's focused enough to lay out his plan and implement it to perfection every time. The latest victim, Mark Fellenz, was a cement mixer, the second person in that type of trade, and worked at Ready-Pour according to our interview with the neighbor. The perp could have been fired from his job and is going after individuals that may have had a beef with his work ethic or personality. He has a short fuse and is easily agitated. His trigger may be the loss of a job, which actually gives him the freedom to follow his victims around any time day or night."

Agent Tam nodded. "That makes sense, Bruce, thank you. Anyone else?"

J.T. thumbed the side of my leg under the table, making me wince, which caught Agent Tam's attention.

"Jade, were you going to add something?"

I looked from her face to Bruce's. "I'm sorry, but I have to disagree with Agent Starks. The loss of a job at a cement company wouldn't have anything to do with Beverly Grant. A cinder block was found at the scene of her murder too, which indicates it's the same killer. There isn't a job connection there. The trigger has to be something else."

"If you have an idea other than the one Agent Starks has, I want to hear it. Go ahead."

"With all due respect, ma'am, this isn't my first rodeo. Yes, I recently became an FBI agent, but I have a lot of experience with different types of killers, including women."

"Women?"

"Yes, ma'am. Granted, statistics say women make up just ten percent of all murderers. Women also act on emotion, especially if the trigger is something close to their heart. I'd picture a murderer that was fired from their job as somebody who would go in with guns blazing, as in the catchphrase of *going postal*." I took a sip of water and gathered my thoughts. "Women are usually more calculating if the reason is personal and if they're seeking retribution. I took several pictures at the victim's home earlier because I knew we wouldn't hear anything from the forensic team by the time this meeting took place. A still-damp impression of a bare foot was on the bathroom rug. It seemed narrower and shorter than what one would expect from the six-foot-two, two-hundred-ten-pound Mark Fellenz."

Agent Tam raised her brows as if in question and leaned hard against the back of her chair. "How do you know his height and weight?"

"Mark's open wallet was on the kitchen counter, and his driver's license was inside, behind the plastic sleeve. I took a look. I'm sure the crime lab can compare the foot size on the rug to Mark's foot size. They could even estimate the imprint's size by the length and width of the bath rug."

I slid my phone across the table to Agent Tam. She picked it up and looked closely.

"The next picture is of a shoe impression on the wall outside a guest room window. We believe that's how the perp gained entrance to the house. Forensics can easily compare the tread pattern to any shoes owned by Mark Fellenz."

sandwich for lunch. Jordan placed a mat under her plate, set the cup of coffee to her right, and pulled out the kitchen chair. She sat and read over her notes then checked the time on her cell phone—four hours left before she'd leave for that appointment with victim number five. She browsed the Internet as she ate and found images of the tools he'd have readily available in his studio. After perusing the landscape architect's website and personal biography, she realized he too was a single man, and her approach for getting into his house was as simple as setting up an appointment to see 3D landscape renderings on his studio computer. Luckily, in the past, Myron Dormin had never met her. His landscape designs were all approved by Kent. The appointment was set for five thirty that day, and she'd have Myron all to herself.

Chapter 16

I was sure anybody that had sued a bricklayer, cement maker, or anyone in the hardscape trades would be listed on the circuit court website for Harris County. It was a good place to start, and we'd get to that as soon as we returned from the police department.

Once we arrived downtown, J.T. and I checked in with the desk sergeant, Lynn Allen, showed our credentials, and asked where we'd find the specific departments we were looking for.

"Both the forensic lab and the coroner's offices are on the lower level. Follow that right hallway"—she pointed— "and you'll find a stairway that will take you down to their offices. There's an arrow at the bottom of the stairs that will show you which way to go."

I thanked her, and we turned at the right hallway and found the steps to the lower level. According to the arrow, the forensic lab was to our left and the coroner's office to our right.

"Want to buddy up or go in individually?" J.T. asked.

"Let's each take a department so we get out of here faster. I'll take forensics, you can have the coroner. All we really need from the coroner is an inked print of Mark's foot. The forensics lab can compare it to the indention on the rug."

"Okay, I'll tell them forensics is waiting for it. Maybe they'll do it right away if that's the case."

We parted ways at the bottom of the stairs, and I headed left. I entered through the double glass doors that had Forensics Lab written across them in black text.

The team leader, Rachel Fry, glanced my way and gave me a smile of recognition.

"Agent Monroe, what can we do for you?"

I didn't want to sound like I was telling them how to do their jobs, but finding out this information was urgent, and it would eliminate the need to search for a male suspect. I put on a friendly 'not here to tell you what to do' face and asked for her immediate assistance.

She took a seat on one of the roller stools and folded her hands in her lap. "Sure, what can we do to help?"

"At the moment, I only need one thing, and it's rather urgent. It will steer our investigation in the right direction so there won't be any time wasted. I believe that damp foot impression on the bath rug belongs to a woman, not Mark Fellenz. He was a large, solid man, and I'd think his weight would have caused a deeper, longer, and wider impression. I hope you guys scaled that print with a ruler when you photographed it."

"I wasn't actually the person that photographed it, Jeff did, but that is protocol."

I followed Rachel across the room to Jeff's station. He was sorting through evidence. I re-introduced myself and told him what I needed.

"Sure thing. I just downloaded all of the evidence photographs from the camera to my computer a few minutes ago." He pointed at a roller stool. "Have a seat."

I sat next to Jeff as he wiggled the computer mouse, pointed the curser at the file he needed, and double clicked. A file consisting of nearly one hundred photos popped up. "Wow, you guys are thorough. That's good to know."

"So, we're looking for the bathroom photo with the imprint on the rug?"

"That's correct." I leaned in while he scanned the rows of pictures left to right. "There they are," I said as I pointed at the pale blue rug on the bathroom floor.

"Yeah, good thing we did scale it. The blue rug almost washes out the image once it's on the computer." Jeff moved the zoom bar to the right and enlarged the picture. "Give me just a minute, please." He crossed the room and picked up a telephone on the nearest desk. "Hey, Marty, do me a favor and measure the length of Mark Fellenz's right foot. Sure, call me back." He returned to the computer and sat down. "The assistant medical examiner is going to measure Mark's foot length. I guess he was in the process of doing it already. One of your agents is in there asking for it." The left side of his lip curled up in a grin. "Double teaming us?"

"Sorry, but it's urgent."

"No worries. Oddly enough, most people tend to think women's feet are just a smaller version of men's feet, but they're actually very different. The distance from the heel to the ball of a man's foot is longer than a woman's, and the width of their feet is greater across the ball region. Women tend to have a higher instep, making their feet look narrower in that area. Once you know the difference, it's easy to spot."

Jeff's comment reminded me of how the male and female pelvic bones were explained to me months back by a crew helping us with an investigation at a farm where human remains were found. Once we saw the difference between them, we would instantly know which were male and which were female.

The phone on the desk rang, and Rachel picked it up.

"Thanks, Marty, I'll let Jeff know." She walked over and told us that Mark's foot was eleven inches long and four and a half inches wide.

Jeff scooted in his chair and looked at the evidence photograph again. "According to the ruler on the photograph, this footprint is about nine by four. Granted, the rug will cause a certain degree of miscalculation, but I'd say with almost certainty that the footprint belonged to a woman. Plus, Mark was found in bed. If he had showered the night before, he would have likely walked over the rug several more times before going to sleep, and it wouldn't be damp anymore."

"You're absolutely right. Thanks, Jeff. There's the shoeprint on the outer wall of the house too. Has anyone compared the tread pattern to Mark's shoes?"

"Not yet, but we did photograph every shoe in the

house. The width of that print leans more toward a woman too, that much I'm sure of."

"Could I take a look at those photographs? It will save me time by not having to go out to the house again."

"Yeah, I'll pull up that folder."

"One more thing, Jeff. Would you mind making your determination official?"

"As in writing it down on paper?"

"Please?"

"Sure, I'll have Rachel do that, no problem."

"Awesome, thanks." I called J.T.'s cell and told him to come into the forensics lab. We had photos to review.

After ten minutes of comparing the print on the outer wall to the eight pair of shoes in Mark's house, we were absolutely certain none matched. We thanked Rachel and Jeff again. I slipped the official document with the forensic team leader's opinion of the footprint into my purse, and we left for the field office. I needed Agent Tam on board so we could focus on the right killer—a woman.

We found Dave and Bruce in the computer lab, talking on their phones. We told them the opinion of the forensic team and suggested we have a quick meeting with Agent Tam to give her the news. Bruce looked hurt.

"Bruce, this isn't personal. We're trained to weed out and apprehend serial killers. The gender is irrelevant. If the footprint evidence hadn't been staring us right in the face, we would have assumed the killer was a man too. We all need to be on the same page with this."

"You're right, Jade. We aren't trained as thoroughly as

you guys are in this particular field. Let's have a quick powwow with the boss so we can get back to work."

I led the way upstairs to the conference room. Dave called Agent Tam's cell and told her we had news. She was on her way.

Within five minutes, Michelle Tam entered the room and stood at the head of the table. "Let's hear it, and I hope it's something we can work with."

I pulled the folded document out of my purse, stood, and leaned across the table. "Here you go, ma'am. I think this says it all. I'd like every one of us to be working together and agree on the person we're searching for. We have to put together the correct profile if we ever want to catch this killer. Personal opinions need to be set aside for now."

I watched her expression as she read the document. "Very good information here. Nice work, Jade. So where are we on everything?"

"J.T. and I compared all of the photos of the shoes in Mark's house against the image of the tread on the outside wall. None matched. It was another way to double-check that the shoe belonged to the intruder, a woman. Forensics agreed on that as well."

"How about toxicology?"

J.T. responded. "The coroner told me the blood work on Beverly Grant and Ted Arneson came back as clean, but Jerry was as drunk as a skunk. Mark's report should be back tomorrow."

She nodded. "Check Jerry's police and forensic report again and look through the photos they took inside the house. Did anyone see beer or liquor set out or a glass or two in the sink? Were there cans or bottles in the trash? If not, he had to go somewhere to get that drunk. He was found dead and mutilated in his house. His hands had been turned into hamburger by the garbage disposal, for God's sake. Round up the neighbors again and see if they know what bars he frequents. If we're lucky, some place may have him on video."

J.T. wrote that down. "I'll get on that right away, Agent Tam."

"Bruce, Dave, what do you have with the phone calls?"

Dave spoke up. "Ready-Pour fired one person in the last year for falsifying their time card. Apparently that person moved to Arizona six months ago. Several other people quit on their own accord but not due to any misconduct."

She turned her head. "Bruce?"

"Cemcom fired six people in the last year. Taking into account they employ four thousand people, makes six seem like small potatoes."

"True, but the reason is what's important."

"Yes, ma'am, and they said they'd have the personnel director call me this afternoon with each of those six people's files."

"Have we started on the lawsuits for either company?"

"Not yet, Agent Tam, but that's next," J.T. said.

"Okay, if that goes nowhere, we need to have both companies pull up every residential account they worked at in the last year." She glanced at the clock above the door. "It's two thirty, so we still have time to get that done by our four o'clock meeting. Let's wrap this up. I want a completed profile to give the PD first thing tomorrow."

We filed back into the computer lab to begin the Internet search of lawsuits in the county for the companies where our victims worked.

"The online search shouldn't take long. We're only dealing with four companies if we check the 9-1-1 operator's call center too," I said.

J.T. spoke up. "The only company that might take some time is Cemcom because of their size."

"Then let's work on them together. Bruce, why don't you and Dave take the others?"

"Yeah, okay."

We each grabbed a computer station and began our search. I tapped my computer keys to pull up the circuit court records for Harris County and entered Cemcom in the search bar.

"Holy crap, I had no idea how large Cemcom was. They have divisions all over the country."

"Let's stick to the Houston facility, Jade. The rest wouldn't make any sense," J.T. said.

"Yeah, you're right. Even locally, they have several plants and multiple departments. I'm just going to type in the address of the main plant and see what pops up."

I supplied all of the necessary information and went back a year. I clicked on the blue enter key and waited. Pages of lawsuits popped up. They covered the entire company as a single entity instead of by location. I groaned with impatience. I decided to browse the pages by the city the suits were filed in. Hopefully the cities were listed in alphabetical order rather than month and year. J.T. searched for the names of females who'd filed the lawsuit. We needed a woman with a residential account who had filed a suit for any reason whatsoever. At least we'd have somewhere to start.

A half hour later, with both of us working only the Cemcom file, we had two residential lawsuits for Houston, neither had been filed by a woman alone, and both had been dismissed a while back.

I read over the first suit, and the findings showed the homeowner and Cemcom had a miscommunication as to when the pool surround would be completed. They agreed on an undisclosed sum, and the suit went away. The second lawsuit, filed by a Kent and Jordan Taylor, gave no information whatsoever and said only that it was unwarranted and dismissed. I slumped back and raked my hands through my hair.

"J.T., how does this work if the perp isn't found in a few days? Milwaukee needs us back at some point, don't they?"

He acknowledged my frustration with a thoughtful smile. "It's usually our team that apprehends the bad guy, Jade, but if time doesn't allow that, we establish a complete profile, release it to the police department, and head home. There are plenty of agents and local law enforcement personnel that will take over the investigation as long as they have a good start from us."

I chuckled. "Okay. I didn't know if I was supposed to send in a change-of-address form to the post office or not."

"I know what you mean, but you'll get used to it, I promise."

We gathered again in the conference room at four o'clock. Agent Tam stood at the end of the table and updated us on her findings.

"I did some digging myself this afternoon. The police department combed the area around the Fellenz house. They interviewed all the neighbors on the block and some extended family throughout the metro area. Like the others, Mark didn't seem to have any enemies." She glanced in my direction. "It sounds like the only person with a temper was Jerry Fosco. Mark went to work every day, got along with his coworkers, and lived a normal, law-abiding life. So what are we missing, people?" She looked at J.T. "Did you find out anything in Jerry's file?"

"There's no mention of open liquor bottles, beer cans in the trash, or anything like that. The forensic photos don't show anything out of place other than at the kitchen sink area where the crime took place."

"Okay, we need to speak to the neighbors again and ask about Jerry's favorite haunts. Anything on the lawsuits?"

"Two that were dismissed at Cemcom," J.T. said.

"Nothing at the other companies," Dave added.

"Ma'am, we can still put together a decent description. Somebody has to know of a female friend or family member that went through a recent tragedy and is acting unusual. We can give the police what we have, hold a press conference, and let Joe Q. Public call in on a tip line. There isn't a 'norm' for a serial killer. None of them, other than the psychopath with a split personality, can go about an everyday, normal life without raising a red flag with somebody."

Anxiety covered Agent Tam's face. "Check out the stories behind the two lawsuits before we give the PD our profile."

"Yes, ma'am, but I have one more idea up my sleeve."

"Go ahead, Jade."

"What we're doing now involves too much guesswork. We don't have an eyewitness, so we can't work with a sketch artist. We don't have a vehicle to put a BOLO out on, and of course, we don't have that all-important name. There is a faster way to pinpoint who we're looking for, and it might work."

Agent Tam looked hopeful.

"Let's get the residential work records for each of the tradesmen and cross-reference them. Since none of these men worked at the same company, the only way to know if they worked on the same project is to compare their work calendars side by side. If the surveyor, cement mixer, and bricklayer went to the same residence for a work order, say within a couple of weeks of each other, well, that in itself should tell us something."

"Okay, call the companies and make sure they fax those work records here before their offices close for the day. Go to Jerry's, Mark's, and Ted's homes and see if you can find calendars, work records, and addresses that related to their jobs. We need something that will tie these men together. Bring anything you find back here first thing in the morning. We need to compare jobsites and notes. Monroe, I want you to go interview the families related to those dismissed lawsuits. Dave, go back to the Fellenz house and see what you can find. J.T., go to Ted's house and talk to the wife. Bruce, scour Jerry Fosco's house and talk to his neighbors about his favorite bars. Look through each house again with a fine-toothed comb, but this time focus on something that could have a work date and address on it."

Chapter 17

We each left in a separate government-issued car and headed to our designated location. My phone rang as I drove. SSA Spelling was calling me.

"Hello, boss."

"Hello, Jade. How's the FBI in Houston treating you?"

I chuckled. "About the same as any law enforcement agency. I do appreciate the nice hotel room and travel stipend, though."

"How's the case coming along?"

"Slowly. I think I've convinced the crew we're looking for a female perp, though."

"Interesting. Are you making headway?"

"I'd say so. I'm pretty confident we can put together a profile tomorrow for the police department. Everyone needs to be on the same page so we can expedite this killer's capture."

"Absolutely. I'm looking forward to hearing the end result. Keep me posted, Jade."

"I will, boss. Good night." I hung up and called Amber since my GPS told me the address of Dan and Ellie Stein was fifteen minutes away. I missed Amber and looked forward to hearing her voice. She answered right away.

"Hey, Jade, I just left work. Everyone was talking about you."

I laughed. "Why?"

"Because they miss you, that's why. I never realized how much this crazy crew loves you."

I smiled from ear to ear. "That really warms my heart."

"So, how's the case coming along?"

"It's a bit stressful. We can't seem to figure out who the serial killer is other than it's a woman. We haven't found a single thing that ties the victims to each other, then of course, having zero witnesses doesn't help."

"Yeah, that sounds tough. A woman, really? That's interesting."

I sighed. "Anyway, how are you, hon? How's life as a deputy? Is your ass getting bigger?" I chuckled at my own memories from years back of worrying that sitting in a cruiser all day would make me fat. That stress was probably what kept me lean.

"My ass is just fine, thank you."

I laughed again. "Are you glad to be in law enforcement? Do you feel like you made the right decision?"

"Of course I do. I've never doubted that. One department at a time and one step at a time will get me to the place I want to be."

"Good attitude, little sister. How are the guys?"

"Like I said, they're all missing you. I don't stand a chance in your shadow."

"You're funny. Okay, I have to go. I'll talk to you tomorrow night. I hope to be back in a couple of days. Night, hon."

"Night, Jade."

I hung up and clicked my right blinker to change lanes. The residence of Dan and Ellie Stein was coming up on my left.

I pulled into their driveway and parked. I stared down at the paver sidewalk and instantly liked it. I put that idea in my bank of to-do-somedays and carried on.

The large painted door wore a fall wreath filled with faux leaves in bright oranges, reds, and yellows. Acorns, hot glued to the leaves, gave it a perfect finishing touch. Pumpkins in three sizes already lined the porch.

I rang the bell and waited.

Mr. Stein came to the door and pulled it open widely. I introduced myself and noticed the look of surprise that covered his face. I imagined an FBI agent arriving at someone's home during the dinner hour wasn't the norm for most folks.

He welcomed me inside, and I told him I'd be brief.

"Ellie, we have a guest."

A thirtysomething woman appeared in the foyer, and Dan explained who I was.

"Of course, please, let's have a seat." She led the way into a comfortable looking family room where Mrs. Stein asked her daughter to turn off the television and find something else to do for a half hour. The girl, who looked about ten, left the room.

"I'm following up on a current case that may involve Cemcom. I noticed that last spring, you filed a lawsuit against them. Can you give me a brief synopsis of what that was about?"

The couple looked at each other in surprise.

"Are we in trouble for something?" the wife asked.

"Not at all, and a brief explanation will be fine."

Dan spoke up. "It was just a timing delay. We wanted the pool work to be complete by April tenth. Ellie's sister planned her engagement party here and hired caterers for the day. There was so much rain the first week of April, everything was delayed even though the signed contract said the work would be completed by the tenth."

"When was it finished?"

"Not until the end of the month. The backyard was such a mess, Ellie's sister found an indoor venue at the last minute. We settled on Cemcom paying for her venue and the meal. It only came to a few thousand dollars."

"The settlement and resolution was amicable?"

"Yeah, I guess. They finished the work, it looks beautiful, and we haven't spoken to them since."

I put away my notepad after writing down the Steins' contact information. I stood and shook their hands. "Okay, that should do it. I'm sorry to interrupt your evening. I'll show myself out."

Back in the car, I programmed the GPS to take me to the next home. A Kent and Jordan Taylor lived about ten minutes away.

I picked up my cell and called J.T. as I drove. With any

luck, he'd find something at Ted Arneson's house that could tie all of these murders together.

The phone rang six times before J.T. answered.

"Oh, there you are. I was about to hang up."

"Sorry, I got distracted for a minute."

"What was the distraction?" My curiosity was now piqued.

"A simple reminder note on a piece of scratch paper that was pinned to a corkboard in the kitchen. Ted's wife said that's where he put everything work related so he wouldn't forget. She said he sometimes did side jobs unrelated to Cornerview Surveying. According to her, he was always taking notes on scratch paper. The corkboard was his way of staying organized. Apparently it didn't raise questions with the police or forensics when they did a walk-through of the house earlier in the week."

"Do you think it's important?" I merged onto the freeway as we talked.

"Well, it looks like it's been pinned to that corkboard for a while. A man's name, occupation, and address are written across it. Maybe they were co-contracting on a project. The wife didn't recognize the name. Hang on, Jade."

I heard J.T. thank the wife, followed by a noise that sounded like a car door slamming.

"Are you leaving now?" I hoped to call it a night after my final interview and have a relaxing dinner and a glass of wine. I was sure my fifty-dollar stipend would cover everything.

"Yeah, I'm backing out of the driveway."

"What's the guy's name, and what does he do?"

"His name is Myron Dormin, and he's a landscape architect. I'm sure his and Ted's professions go hand in hand."

"True, so now what?"

"I looked the guy up online and called the number. He's self-employed and has a studio in his house. He told me he had an appointment scheduled in a half hour, so I promised to keep my visit short. Anyway, I'm heading over there now. He doesn't live far from the Arneson house, only fifteen minutes to the east, otherwise I would have done a phone interview."

I envisioned a fast-food dinner becoming my evening reality, minus the glass of wine.

"Yeah, I understand. I still have an interview to do myself. Do you want me to wait on dinner so we can go over the case together?"

He laughed into the phone. "Well, I know I'm starving, so you must be too. I'll let you make that call. This should only take me an additional twenty minutes."

"Okay, then, if I get back before you, I'll be waiting at the restaurant bar."

"Fair enough. See you soon."

I clicked off and smiled. I liked J.T. He wasn't uptight or intense. So far, I read him as calm, levelheaded, and kind, although I hadn't seen him in an intense situation—yet.

Chapter 18

Jordan was undecided about swapping out the vehicles. All-Store was twenty minutes away, but Myron Dormin's home was just a six-minute drive. She decided to be cautious, take her personal car, and park under the cover of darkness.

Improvising, Jordan picked up a cinder block from the rubble along the side of the house and placed it on the backseat floor of her car. She double-checked Myron's phone number and address then set the GPS before backing out of the driveway.

A dark sedan caught her eye when it stopped at the curb. Jordan watched through the driver's side mirror. A tall, slender female got out and headed her way.

She lowered the window and killed the engine.

"Good evening, ma'am. My name is Agent Jade Monroe, and I'm with the FBI. Are you Jordan Taylor?"

"Yes, of course. FBI? What can I help you with? I'm actually in a hurry. I just received a call that my sister is in the hospital."

"I'm sorry, ma'am, but I promise to only take a few

minutes of your time. I know you and your husband filed a lawsuit against Cemcom earlier this past spring."

"Cemcom? Yes, but the suit didn't go anywhere. The claims expert came out and evaluated the scene. He said we had nothing to go forward with. The initial proceedings were started, but my husband agreed to drop it."

"Can you tell me what it was about?"

"Agent Monroe, I really need to leave."

"Just one more minute."

Jordan heaved a disgruntled sigh. "We had a retaining wall built that fell over, causing extensive damage. The inspector that represented Cemcom said nobody was to blame and the wall had been built correctly. He blamed it on the overabundance of rain last April. Now please, I have to go."

"Where is your husband, ma'am?"

"He's a medical sales rep and travels a lot. He isn't expected home until Sunday." Jordan turned the key in the ignition. "Are we done now?"

"Yes, I suppose. Drive carefully and mind the speed limit."

Jordan backed out of the driveway and took off down the street. She watched for headlights following her out, but all she saw was darkness.

Less than ten minutes later, Jordan turned in to a sprawling neighborhood with upscale custom homes. Every home had an expansive yard of an acre or more. She appreciated the fact that fewer eyeballs on his house would make slipping away far easier.

Nighttime came early in fall, and the sun had already gone down. Blackness took over as she crept forward. Her car's headlights bounced off the immaculate lawns of those upper-class homes. The robotic GPS voice called out that she had reached her destination. Jordan pulled into the last driveway on the block—the home with the best yard, fitting for somebody in that field of work. She killed the lights and the engine then retrieved the cinder block from the backseat and hid it within the shrubbery near the front door.

She brushed the cement dust off the front of her jacket then smoothed her long blond hair and tucked the wayward strands behind her ears. She removed her glasses and placed them in her left jacket pocket before she rang the bell— nearly a half hour early.

Each approaching footstep sounded louder as he neared the door. She waited and smoothed her hair a final time. Through the beveled glass, she saw Myron Dormin. He pulled the door open, and a pleased expression covered his face. His smile accentuated his dimples, and he stretched out a welcoming hand.

"You must be Jordan Green. Welcome to Dormin Landscape Designs. Did we get the time wrong?"

"No, and I apologize for being early, but I was nearby."

He smiled again. "No worries. Pardon my stare, but you're quite tall for a woman."

"I've heard that before, and yes to your next question. I was a basketball star in college." She chuckled coquettishly through her lies about those nonexistent college years and the made-up last name.

Jordan turned heads, not only because she exceeded six feet in height but also because she was a strikingly beautiful thirty-three-year-old woman. Beauty had one purpose and one purpose only in her mind—to distract those killers long enough to exact revenge on them. Her beautiful face was the tool that got her through many doors.

"Please, come in. My studio is this way." Myron turned left beyond the foyer.

Jordan followed a few steps back while her eyes darted left and right for a tool of opportunity. She dipped her hand in the right jacket pocket and felt the shape of the stun gun.

"So, you're looking to change the landscape of your backyard. Is that correct?"

"Yes, and I'm anxious to see your work."

"Certainly, here we are." He motioned to the guest chair next to his computer. "Please, have a seat. Would you like me to take your coat?"

"No, thanks, I'm fine."

"Okay, I've designed three mock-ups for you. Of course, they're just something to start with. I can change anything as we go along."

Except what you've already done. It's too late for that. You can't take it back.

Jordan glanced at the geometry tools on his drafting table—one in particular caught her eye. She smiled. Maybe she wouldn't need the stun gun after all.

"Excuse me for just a second while I get the printouts."

Myron momentarily left the room, which gave Jordan barely enough time to grab what she needed off the drafting table. She slipped on the latex gloves and took her seat with only seconds to spare. Myron reentered the studio.

"Here we go. These are for you to take home." He placed the printouts on the desk. "Now, let's get to the meat and potatoes." He chuckled and clicked a few computer keys. A 3-D rendering of different backyard styles popped up on the screen.

Jordan thumbed the tool in her pocket and made some adjustments as she secured it in her hand.

"Oh my word, those images are amazing." She leaned in closer, barely inches from Myron's face and felt his hot breath against her cheek.

In one fast thrust, she plunged the sharp metal spike of the geometry compass into his right temple. Blood sprayed out with each heartbeat as Myron flailed and tried to pull the tool from his head.

"I don't think so." She spun his chair and pulled his arms, wrenching his shoulders backward unnaturally until he went limp. "Finally. You murderer."

As she released his arms, his body slid off the chair and dropped to the floor. The stretching snap of the gloves being pulled off sent blood spatter across the computer screen. With the gloves turned inside out, Jordan balled them up and slipped them into her pocket then put on a clean pair. She wasn't about to leave behind fingerprints or a blood evidence trail. She ran out the front door and grabbed the cinder block from behind the bushes. Back in the studio, she assumed he was already dead, but her point still needed to be made. Jordan held the block level with her chest and directly above his head then released it. The crunching impact of his skull being split in half reminded her of cracking open an egg shell. She knelt down and made sure the compass was still in his temple then looked at her jacket in disgust—blood spray coated it. With the jacket off and turned inside out, she slipped her glasses back on and deleted the file Myron had made for her on his computer. With the folder and printouts in hand, along with his daily planner, she exited the house and climbed into her car. As Jordan backed out of the driveway and turned the wheel, a set of approaching headlights nearly blinded her. She pulled the visor down to block the beam as she sped away. With one last glance in the rearview mirror before she turned the corner, Jordan saw the vehicle pull into Myron Dormin's driveway.

Chapter 19

J.T. shifted into park and killed the engine then stepped out of the cruiser. He scanned the lush landscape as he followed the sidewalk to the front door. He pressed the doorbell. Through the door's glass, he saw the illuminated foyer lights. He waited for the sound of footsteps, but they never came. J.T. pressed the bell again and continued to wait. Assuming that nobody was coming to the door, he pulled out his phone and called Dormin Landscape Designs. No answer—voicemail picked up.

That's weird. I talked to him less than a half hour ago.

Not quite sure what to do, J.T. grasped the doorknob and gave it a turn. The door swung open, and he cautiously peeked in. That eerie silence sent a chill up his spine when he called out to Myron and got no response. He felt the cold steel of his service weapon and pulled it out of the holster as he walked through the foyer. Straight ahead lay a large great room—it was vacant. Hallways veered right and left. He chose left only because lights were on in that direction. With his head on a swivel, J.T. hugged the wall and pushed forward slowly, his gun drawn and against his chest in case of an ambush. He had no idea whether someone lay in wait, and each room needed to be cleared before he continued to the next. A quick peek around the corner showed the first room on the left to be an office. A large desk, bookcase, and printer on a credenza filled the space. The room appeared undisturbed, but the blinking light on the printer caught his attention. He continued on and checked the next room across the hall—a powder room, and it was clear.

"Mr. Dormin, are you here?" Still no answer.

Two more doors were down that hallway. One definitely entered into a room, and the other could be a closet, he thought as he compared door sizes. J.T. looked around the doorframe to a scene he wouldn't easily forget. A body, who he assumed was Myron Dormin, lay on the floor, his head smashed beneath a cinder block and clearly dead. A quick sweep of the room showed no evidence of anyone else there.

"Son of a bitch." J.T. dialed Jade, knowing she could round up the right group of people quickly while he continued to clear the house. As he knelt with his fingertips on the man's wrist and listened to Jade's phone ring, J.T. felt for a pulse. There wasn't one.

"Hi, J.T. I'm at the hotel bar. What's your ETA?"

"Jade, I need the police and our group at Myron Dormin's residence immediately. I just arrived and found a dead man lying on the floor. The scene is pretty gruesome. I haven't even cleared the house yet, but by the looks of the body with a cinder block buried in his skull, I'm assuming it's Myron Dormin. Here's the address. Get everyone out here as fast as possible."

"Holy shit, I'm on it. I'll get the nearest police department there first. Be careful, J.T."

"Yep, I will." He clicked off and continued cautiously through the house.

Chapter 20

I quickly made the 9-1-1 call, gave them the address, and then scrolled through my phone contacts to find Michelle Tam's number. I told her that J.T. needed the downtown forensic team and ME at the home of Myron Dormin. After hanging up with her, I called Bruce and Dave. A quick explanation and the address was all they needed. With my bar tab settled, I grabbed the keys for the cruiser I had used earlier, signed the car out, slipped on my FBI jacket, and programmed the address into my GPS. From the hotel, the distance showed a fifteen-minute drive.

I arrived at the residence where police cars flooded the driveway and street. Red and blue lights flickered on every squad car. The perimeter of the property had already been cordoned off with yellow tape. Several officers stood guard to keep the growing number of looky-loos at bay. I parked along the curb, showed my badge to an officer, and slipped under the tape. J.T.'s cruiser was among the four cars parked in the driveway. The forensics and coroner's vans were already there. I followed the sidewalk to the well-lit house and met another officer at the front door. He allowed me to enter.

Inside, part of the forensic team was hard at work, dusting for prints and taking pictures. The mayhem seemed to be down the left hallway by the quantity of people gathered in that area. I reached the bottleneck that spilled out into the hallway from one room. From what I saw over a few shoulders, the group included J.T., more of the forensic team, several officers, and the ME. Other than J.T., I hadn't caught a glimpse of any other colleagues or Agent Tam yet.

From behind my back, I heard the familiar no-nonsense voice of Michelle Tam barking out commands. Officers moved aside as she pushed her way through the crowd. I hadn't made it into the room myself when she reached me.

"Agent Monroe, what do we have?"

"I can't tell, ma'am. I haven't made it through the crowd yet."

"Excuse us. Please move aside and let us through." She made her presence known, as any high-ranking FBI agent would. The crowd parted, allowing us a small pathway to squeeze through. The sight in front of us was as J.T. described—gruesome.

J.T. nodded and walked over when he saw us. "Agent Tam, Jade, we've got a real mess here."

"What do you make of it, other than the obvious block on the man's head?" Agent Tam asked.

J.T. jerked his chin toward the body. "I'm sure the blow on the head was the kill shot, but take a look at this."

He led us alongside the body and knelt down. We

gloved up and did the same. A blood-coated drafting compass was jammed deep into the man's temple.

"Has forensics photographed everything in here?" Agent Tam asked.

George Craig, the senior ME, spoke up. "Not yet, just the body, but now I can proceed while they continue with the rest of the room. My hands were tied until they finished photographing every angle of the deceased."

"Understood." Agent Tam nodded. "Go ahead, George."

With gloved hands, the ME lifted the cinder block off the head of the victim and sucked in a deep breath. "Not a pretty sight."

"That's a fact," J.T. said. "George, would you mind checking for a wallet so we can rule out the possibility of this man being anyone besides Myron Dormin?"

"Sure thing, Agent Harper." George patted the pant pockets of the deceased and felt the shape of a wallet in the rear left pocket. "Here we go." He lifted the man's hip and slid the wallet out then flipped the trifold open. He nodded and handed the wallet to J.T.

J.T. double-checked the name and address on the driver's license as well as the description of the man. As it stood, the photo didn't help. "By the description," J.T. said, "it's definitely Myron Dormin. He had to have been killed minutes before I arrived."

George jerked his head toward the wall clock. "Judging by the time right now, I'd say he was killed less than a half hour ago. His body is still warm to the touch."

J.T. nodded. "Yeah, that makes sense and—"

I blurted out a *What?* after seeing a surprised expression on J.T.'s face. It was obvious he'd just remembered something.

"Son of a bitch. This is the last house on the block, correct?"

A nearby officer confirmed that it was.

J.T. whispered for us to join him as he stood up and crossed the room. The four of us followed and huddled against the corner wall with him.

"What's going on, Agent Harper?" Agent Tam asked.

J.T. kept his voice low. "When I got here, I passed a car coming toward me from the end of the street. It had to be the killer if there aren't any houses beyond this one. Damn it. I missed the attack by mere seconds."

"Consider yourself lucky. By the way each of the crime scenes looked, that killer is no joke," Dave Miller said.

"Did you get a look at the car?" I asked, even though I knew how dark the area was other than the ambient glow of house lights and the occasional street lamp. I pulled out my notepad, just in case.

He rubbed his brow, as if in thought. "It wasn't a compact car or a sports car. My best guess would be a darker sedan. I mean, my headlamps were directly on it, but I wasn't focused on the car. I was looking for the house number. There was something else too, but what was it?" J.T. contorted his face into a frown as he seemed to be rewinding his thoughts. "That's right, it was what Myron said while I was on the phone with him." J.T. looked around to make sure nobody was eavesdropping. "He told me he had an appointment soon. He excused himself from the phone to look up the time. Through the phone line, I heard pages shuffle, then Myron mumbled out loud 'Jordan Green at five thirty.' He came back to the phone and told me the time of his appointment."

"Then where is this Jordan Green?" I checked my watch—6:00. "And what are the odds of two people named Jordan in one night?"

"That is odd. Did Myron give you any indication of Jordan being male or female?"

"No, not at all, and that name could go either way."

Agent Tam continued. "I'm sure the officers turned away all cars coming down the street that weren't in law enforcement." She looked at J.T. "Do you remember exactly what time you arrived here?"

"Later than I had hoped. I'm thinking around five twenty."

"And what time did you speak to Mr. Dormin on the phone?" Agent Tam nodded at me to write down everything as J.T. recalled it.

J.T. raised his brow. "It was just before Agent Monroe called me. I was actually getting ready to leave Ted Arneson's house." He looked at me. "So that was?"

I checked my call logs. "Five after five is when I called you."

He scratched the stubble on his chin. "Yeah, that sounds right. So in the span of fifteen to twenty minutes' time, the killer was able to do all of this devastation. That takes precise planning and execution."

"Let's head back to the field office. Sorry, guys, but this takes priority over relaxation," Agent Tam said. "I'll order dinner to be brought in."

Chapter 21

We gathered in the conference room again. I had seen more of that space than my own hotel room in the last few days. Agent Tam must have called ahead for someone to bring coffee up to the conference room. Two thermal carafes and a stack of cups sat in the middle of the table when we arrived.

"Let's get started, people. I've taken the liberty of ordering several large pizzas. They'll be here soon, and it looks like that's dinner for tonight." Agent Tam pulled the ring on the drop-down whiteboard that was attached to the wall behind the table. With a marker in hand, she was ready to write. "Let's begin with what we know to be true. Somebody is taking out each of these people with a cinder block or cement. The murder weapon has to represent some type of injustice in the killer's mind, and each of these victims was chosen deliberately."

J.T. spoke up. "I heard Myron mention the name Jordan Green, and Jade interviewed a Jordan Taylor within forty-five minutes of the murder."

"What about the officers turning away cars approaching Myron's house?"

Dave Miller spoke up. "I asked when we left the scene. None of the officers turned away a vehicle."

Agent Tam wrote that on the whiteboard. "Tell us about Jordan Taylor, Jade."

I let out an exhausted breath and cleared my head. "Okay, I approached the home and saw brake lights flash in the driveway. It appeared that somebody was leaving the residence. I walked up to the car, and the woman inside identified herself as Jordan Taylor. I asked for a few minutes of her time and brought up the lawsuit. She seemed rushed, but she did tell me her sister was in the hospital, and that's where she was heading. What I got out of her was that the lawsuit against Cemcom was never officially filed. Apparently they had a retaining wall built that collapsed after a week of heavy rain. The claims specialist that came out on behalf of Cemcom told them they didn't have a valid complaint against the company. He said they couldn't sue for damages because of weather issues. It was just a freak accident."

"Was the husband with her?" Agent Tam asked.

"Nope, she said he was out of town. Apparently he's a medical sales rep and travels a lot."

"What kind of car was she in, and what did she look like?" J.T. asked.

I nodded, knowing what he was getting at. "She did have a dark sedan, but I didn't think to check the make and model. She never got out, so I couldn't tell you her height or weight. She had long blond hair, though. From what I could see in the dark, she looked to be between thirty and forty."

"Dave, pull up her driver's license."

"You got it, boss. I mean, Agent Tam."

A slight smile crossed her lips. "Boss is fine."

Dave exited the room and took the elevator to the computer lab. He was back in the conference room ten minutes later with a printout of Jordan Taylor's driver's license and registration. He slid it across the table to Agent Tam.

I watched her expression change. "The registration says she drives a dark blue 2009 Accord." She gave me a glance. "Does that fit the description of the car she was sitting in?"

I agreed with a nod. "I'd go with that, boss."

"J.T., what about the car you saw near the Dormin house?"

"An Accord would work."

"Good, now we're getting somewhere." She looked at the printout of Jordan's driver's license and smiled. "According to her license, it says Jordan Taylor is thirty-three years old, weighs one hundred sixty-two pounds, and she's six foot one inch."

I nearly leaped from my chair. "Is everyone thinking the same thing I am?"

"That Jordan Taylor and Jordan Green are one and the same?" Bruce said.

"We need to get a search warrant. Chances are, we can match that shoe tread on the wall of Mark's house to a pair of shoes she owns," I said.

Agent Tam poured a round of coffee. "Jade, take a breath. A search warrant takes a judge's approval and signature, and then there's the fact that tomorrow starts the weekend. We need something more. Right now we're just speculating with no conclusive evidence to go along with our theories. We don't have proof of anything."

Seconds later, the landline phone in the conference room rang. Agent Tam picked it up.

"SSA Michelle Tam speaking. How may I help you?"

She told us that Rachel from the forensics lab was calling.

"Rachel, I'm putting you on speakerphone. Go ahead."

"Good evening, Agent Tam. I wanted to let you know the blood work from Mark Fellenz just arrived. The ME already left for the night, and he asked if I'd relay the results to you when they came in. Apparently, Mark Fellenz was injected with Methohexital."

"Methohexital? That's a new one."

"Boss?"

"Yes, Jade."

"Jordan Taylor may have access to that drug. She did say her husband is a medical sales rep."

Agent Tam nodded. "Rachel, who has access to that type of drug? It is a controlled substance, isn't it?"

"It absolutely is, ma'am, and other than pharmacies, hospitals, and doctors, I guess only drug reps could get their hands on it legally."

"Good to know. Thanks for the update, Rachel." She hung up and gave each of us a grin. "We're making progress, guys." She wrote that bit of information on the whiteboard. "Okay, what about Jerry Fosco's neighbors, Bruce?"

"Damn, with all this commotion, I almost forgot. The guy two houses down the street said Jerry bugged him a number of times about going to TaTas with him. He swears he never did because his wife would have killed him."

"TaTas? Clever name. Is that what I think it is, a strip club?"

"Apparently so, ma'am."

Agent Tam's cell phone buzzed on the table. She checked the text then addressed J.T. with two twenties in her hand. "Would you mind running downstairs and bringing the pizzas up? The deliveryman is at the reception counter. Let's break for dinner and continue this conversation after we eat."

Chapter 22

Jordan was back in the safe solitude of her home. That alone time was the only way she had the opportunity to do what needed to be done. She could never pull off these heinous crimes if Kent was around. Jordan sat on the couch, a glass of wine at her side, as she scrolled through Myron's cell phone and deleted every communication between them. Even if the police subpoenaed his records, they could never tie him to her, or any of the victims, for that matter. Her prepaid phone gave her complete anonymity.

The jacket she wore earlier lay submerged in a sink of cold water in the laundry room. She hoped the blood stains would wash away, or she'd have to burn it.

With every conversation now erased, she tossed Myron's phone into the microwave and set the timer for ten minutes. She had seen somebody do that on a made-for-TV crime series and wanted to know if it would really destroy the phone. With the paperwork she'd taken from the Dormin house lying in the trash can, Jordan struck a match and tossed it in. Flames burst upward and set his daily calendar, along with Ted Arneson's, on fire. She opened a few windows and poured another glass of wine.

Myron's name was checked off her list—five down and three to go. The end of the retribution was right around the corner, and she wouldn't stop until they were all dead.

With the wineglass in one hand and the legal pad in the other, Jordan looked at the next name on her list. Numbers one through eight were written on the left side of the paper with a corresponding name assigned to each number.

The hatred she felt for John Nels, the inspector that had looked over the crumbled retaining wall, took her back to that dark place. That was the day he told her she didn't have a claim against Cemcom, or anybody, for that matter. She'd never win the lawsuit. Days of constant rain and saturated ground caused the horrific accident—nothing more. She looked forward to ending John Nels's life. In her mind, everyone skated by scot-free and admitted no responsibility whatsoever. Each person and every company got a pass on his word alone.

That won't do, now will it, John? I'll have to come up with something suitable for you.

She stared at the last two names on the sheet and smiled.

Killing you two will give me the most satisfaction of all. I'm saving the best for last.

Chapter 23

I wolfed down my last piece of pizza about the same time everyone else did. A beer would have gone nicely with it, but like it or not, we were still on the clock.

Agent Tam suggested the guys go to TaTas to look over the surveillance camera feed from Monday night. If Jerry was there that night, and as drunk as the toxicology report stated he was, he certainly didn't drive himself home. He also had stun gun marks on his neck that were identical to the ones Beverly Grant and Ted Arneson had.

I ribbed the guys about being chosen to visit TaTas. I had my own agenda to concentrate on so I headed to the computer lab to look up every medical sales company in the metro Houston area to see what I could find. I needed to speak to Kent Taylor as soon as possible. Maybe he could enlighten me about his wife's personality. That brief conversation I had with Jordan didn't tell me enough. If she was the killer, I still didn't know her trigger.

I turned around when the door opened at my back. J.T. entered with a Styrofoam cup of steaming coffee. "Thought you might need this after all the pizza you ate."

I was getting acquainted with the playful side of J.T., and I liked it. "Meaning what? That I'd fall asleep after eating? That's more of a guy thing, and the pizza wasn't quite a Thanksgiving dinner." I grinned. "Appreciate it, though. I thought you were going with Bruce and Dave."

"I am. They had to hit the john first. We'll be leaving soon."

"I think I'll work for an hour and call it a night. I could use a decent night's sleep."

"Yeah, I hear that."

"So, I'm stuck on how our killer subdued Myron Dormin. He was the only one without a stun gun mark on his body." I raked my hands through my hair. "I'm thinking she showed up early, and he wasn't prepared yet. That would explain why we didn't find any mock-ups, printouts, or price sheets. There wasn't even a file for her on his computer, according to forensics."

J.T. scratched his chin. "Makes sense. She caught him off guard when he was trying to get organized and nailed him literally in the temple with that compass."

Bruce and Dave walked in seconds later.

"Ready?" Dave asked as he jerked his head toward the door.

"Yep, let's go."

"Hey, don't have too much fun, guys. You're supposed to be serious FBI agents, you know."

I worked for another thirty minutes and printed out names of all the medical sales companies in the area. I leaned back in my chair and thought about Jordan's words. The retaining wall toppled over. If there were any blocks left, it could be a way of comparing hers to the ones used in the murders. There had to be some sort of science that could tell us if the blocks used as murder weapons came from the same lot as ones that possibly remained at her home. I wanted to take a look for myself. With the last gulp of coffee to wake myself up, I checked out a car and left for the Taylor residence.

I tried J.T.'s phone as I drove. Past experience told me it wasn't wise to go to a possible murderer's house and snoop around alone. I was sure Dave and Bruce could handle checking out the video at TaTas on their own. The call dropped every time I dialed his number. I stared at my phone, shook it several times, and even tapped it against the dashboard, but nothing helped. I couldn't get through to him.

Damn it. What's wrong with the cell service tonight? Even if his phone is off, I should still be able to leave a message.

I decided to continue on and take a harmless peek. Nobody would be the wiser, and I had no intentions of knocking on Jordan's door. I just wanted a quick look around the yard.

The clock on the dashboard showed nine o'clock by the time I pulled onto her street and parked a few houses down, where the area was absent of street lamps. The black sedan was nearly invisible along the curb. I'd be there and gone in a matter of minutes. Slivers of light peeked around the edges of the drawn drapes in what was likely the living room. She was probably still up unless she left lights on when Kent was away.

I crept along the outside edge of the driveway and turned at the side of the garage. I looked for an area on the property that would have had a retaining wall out of necessity or purely for ornamentation. A quick flick of my flashlight every few feet sufficed as I did a wide sweep between the houses. The neighbor's yard appeared to stand at a higher elevation, and the ground between the properties looked washed away. That had to be where the retaining wall once stood. I turned and shined my flashlight toward the side of the house, then I saw them. Stacks of whole and broken cinder blocks lined the wall at the end of the garage. I needed only one to take back with me, and I was sure nobody would miss it. I held the flashlight between my teeth and pulled one block away from the stack. Stones toppled to the ground and hit the walkway that wrapped the side yard. The sound was too loud to go unnoticed. I grimaced and turned with the block under my arm. I had hopes of making a quick exit when the blinding light hit me square in the face. The voice was unmistakable. Jordan Taylor had caught me in the act.

"Evening, Agent Monroe. I see you've come back."

The sound of the electric current bouncing between the prongs buzzed in my head, and the pain was excruciating. My knees buckled under me, and I hit the ground.

Chapter 24

"I was minding my own business and enjoying a glass of wine, until I heard that sound outside. Good thing I forgot to close the windows earlier, but now I have to deal with your sorry ass."

Jordan stared down at the agent's writhing body then grabbed her by the arms and dragged her to the garage. She entered the code and slipped under the rising door. With Jade's sidearm removed and safely placed on the workbench, Jordan zip-tied her hands and feet together then jammed a rag into her mouth to keep her quiet. She scoured the workbench until she found a roll of duct tape. With the edge pinched between her teeth, she ripped off a strip and secured it over Jade's mouth.

"Now what the hell am I supposed to do with you? This wasn't in my plans, you stupid bitch." Jordan kicked Jade in the ribs then paced back and forth in the garage. "Where's your cell phone? That has to go."

She dug through Jade's pockets until she felt the shape of the phone. She pulled it out, turned it off, and stomped it on the cement floor.

"I've got to get rid of the car you came in before anything else." She dug again and found the set of keys in Jade's right back pocket. "I have to think this through. There's no way in hell you're going to disrupt my plans."

Jordan exited the garage through the side door and clicked the key fob to the car. She saw lights blink on a vehicle a few houses away. She jogged to the cruiser, got in, and with the lights off, backed into the driveway. She entered the garage the same way she exited then dragged Jade to the corner, raised the overhead, and drove the cruiser in. Jordan slammed the car door behind her as she climbed out, then she slapped the button on the wall and lowered the overhead. She heaved a deep sigh and gave the agent a hateful scowl as she headed into the house.

"Why couldn't you have left me alone?"

Minutes later, Jordan returned to the garage with a syringe in hand. She pulled off the cap and sank the needle into Jade's arm then watched as Jade's eyelids became heavy and finally closed.

"Now to get rid of you, the cinder blocks, and everything in the house that could be used against me."

With the trunk popped and the side door open, Jordan filled the trunk with every block that was stacked outside. Back in the house with a garbage bag in hand, she filled it with her unused medications, latex gloves, notes, phone, tax and bank receipts, and everything she had hidden that belonged to those despicable people. She gave the house a final once-over then returned to the garage. With Jade's service weapon tucked in her purse, her broken phone in the cup holder, and the car ready to go, she lifted the agent from the floor and dropped her in the backseat of the cruiser. She pulled out of the garage and headed to the All-Store facility.

Jordan watched her surroundings as she drove. Driving a car with government-issued plates was a risk she had to take. Constant checks through the side mirrors kept her on edge but alert. She flicked her second cigarette out the window and tossed Jade's phone out too. Twenty minutes later and without incident, she slipped her card into the slot, the gate lifted, and she drove through. She backed the cruiser as close to the roller door as possible and killed the engine. Quickly, even though the facility was as dead and quiet as a cemetery, Jordan emptied the car's contents into the garage then pulled the unconscious agent out, lifted her over her shoulder, and deposited her in the back of the van. With a click of the fob, Jordan locked the van and exited the garage. She pulled the roller door down and turned the key in the lock, then she gave the handle a tug to make sure it was secure and drove out of the facility. She knew the perfect place to dispose of the cruiser, and it could buy her a few extra days.

Sounds of jets lined up on the runway, their engines revving, echoed in her ears as she pulled into the short-term lot at the airport a half hour later. She locked the cruiser's doors, dropped the keys into the nearest trash can, and took the sidewalk to the arrivals area where she flagged down a taxi.

"Where to, ma'am?" the driver asked as Jordan climbed into the backseat.

"The intersection of Fairmont and Clark will do just fine."

"You got it. Have a nice flight?"

"Let's just say it was an unexpected trip."

Jordan leaned back in the seat and closed her eyes. The drive would take twenty minutes.

"We're here, ma'am," the driver said as he pulled to the curb.

With closed fists, Jordan rubbed the sleep out of her eyes, handed him thirty dollars, and exited the cab. An eight-block walk would get her back to her front door.

Chapter 25

The pounding bass of the deep sultry music mixed with occasional hoots and hollers had become distracting.

"Can we please close that door?" J.T. asked as he became increasingly annoyed.

"Sorry, man, I'm the head of security. I have to keep an eye on the stage and bar area."

"I bet you do," Bruce said as he rolled his eyes.

J.T. redirected the men back to the video footage on the computer screen. "Is that the best clarity you can get of the parking lot? It's so grainy you can't make out anyone's features."

"Complain to the owner. This equipment is at least fifteen years old. Upgrading is expensive, and to be honest, we've never had anyone ask to see our tapes."

Dave groaned. "I'm sure by the crowd you pull in, the owner could easily afford new equipment. Everything is way too dark on this tape, inside and out."

John Lissome, the head of security, had become testy and apparently tired of the three FBI goons wasting the last hour of his time. "Dude, this *is* a strip club. The only thing that's ever lit up is the stage. I'm sure you noticed that when you boys walked through."

"Okay, take a breath. Let's check that parking lot footage again," J.T. said.

"You mean for the sixth time?"

J.T. glared. "Yeah, that's exactly what I mean. Do you have a problem with it?"

The man sighed. "I need to get back to my job, that's all."

"In due time. Now rewind that tape and run it at a slower speed." After reviewing the tape again with nothing definitive showing up, J.T. stood and ground his fist into his eyes. "We'll need to take that tape with us. The downtown PD's tech department might be able to clean it up." He handed John Lissome his business card and asked him to pull the tape.

"The owner isn't going to be happy about this."

"I thought you just said nobody has ever asked to see any tapes in the past. Why would it matter now? Do you really want to interfere with an ongoing investigation?"

"No, but—"

"But what? I just gave you my card. If you feel the need to squeal yourself out to the owner, go ahead and share my phone number. I'm sure we can find a few violations in this fine establishment of his. You'll get the tape back soon enough. Now let's have it."

John pulled the tape and handed it to J.T. The men exited the building and left TaTas beating music behind.

"Do you think that grainy image was really of Jerry and Jordan?" Bruce asked during the ride downtown.

J.T. shrugged. "I can't say for sure. Never saw Jerry or Jordan in the flesh. We don't know their mannerisms or their gait, but if the tech department can clean up the footage, we may have hope. According to Jordan's driver's license, she's over six feet tall. Do either of you know Jerry's height?"

Dave spoke up. "No, but we can easily get it from the coroner. We'll be in the same building, anyway."

J.T. parked the sedan on the street. They took the sidewalk to the front of the building, where the police department was located. The downtown police headquarters, tech department, forensics department, and coroner's office and morgue shared the lower level and first floor of the three-story cement building. The upper floor held the city administrative offices and the downtown library. Across the street stood the fire department.

The men entered the building and approached the counter. With a flash of his FBI badge through the plastic window of a leather bifold ID holder, J.T. explained to the evening desk sergeant how they needed the help of the tech department and the coroner.

"The coroner has left for the evening, but I believe Marty Lowrey is here. Just follow that hallway—"

J.T. politely interrupted. "Thanks, we know the way."

Downstairs, the men entered the tech department with the tape in hand.

"Hang out here and tell them what we need. I'm going to check in with Marty," J.T. said.

Dave nodded and went on to explain how grainy the videotape was. They needed it cleaned up the best way possible.

J.T. followed the opposite hallway to the coroner's office. Through the wall of glass, he saw Marty with his chair snugged in tightly against his desk, going over a stack of paperwork. J.T. knocked on the window to get his attention.

With a smile of recognition and a wave, Marty welcomed J.T. in.

"Don't you guys ever take a break?" he asked with a look of surprise. The clock showed it was nearly 11 p.m. "How can I help you, Agent Harper?"

"I like being informal. J.T. is fine. I need to know how tall Jerry Fosco was."

"Sure thing. Give me one second to pull up his file." Marty tapped a few computer keys and opened up the file containing the autopsy report for Jerry Fosco. He leaned in and read the document. "Here we go. It appears that Jerry Fosco was—" He pulled out his calculator and smiled. "Everything is recorded in metric, you know. I never did understand that given the fact that we're in the United States. Okay, his height converts to five foot nine inches."

J.T. raked his fingertips across his beard stubble. "I don't know if that helps me or not."

"What's the problem?"

"We're trying to compare the height of two people in a surveillance tape, walking side by side. We aren't sure if it's Jerry and a woman in question that naturally stands over six feet tall. Women tend to wear heels when they go out, which would throw off her height considerably."

"Then wouldn't she tower over him regardless of if she had on heels or not?"

"True, but the woman could be five foot six and wearing seven-inch heels."

"I see your point. Maybe the tech department can help figure that out."

J.T. nodded and exited the room. "Thanks, Marty," he said and closed the door at his back. He walked the opposite way down the hall and entered the tech department to find everyone huddled around a computer. Mike Walters and Jason Branch manned the night shift.

"Any luck?" Dave asked as J.T. grabbed a vacant chair and pulled up alongside the rest of the crew.

"Jerry Fosco was five foot nine. How's it going with the tape?"

"Slowly," Bruce said. "We can tell the person on the left has long blond hair, so we're assuming it's Jordan. There's something weird going on, though. The man seems to be walking unnaturally. Did Jerry have a leg problem?"

"Not to my knowledge, but don't forget he was way beyond the legal limit that night."

Dave nodded. "That's right."

Mike Walters sighed. "We aren't going to get this tape much better, guys. The image quality really sucks. No matter what, it's doubtful if this is usable footage. You don't have anyone facing the camera, and even if you did, it's too grainy to make a positive ID."

"How about the car they're walking to? That's a larger image to focus on."

Jason zoomed in on the car whose lights flashed when the couple approached it. He turned several knobs to adjust the clarity.

"All I can tell is that it's a light-colored sedan. The boxy shape would lean more toward a car over ten years old. That's all we can help you with, agents. Sorry." He pressed the eject button and handed J.T. the tape. "Tell those guys to get with the twenty-first century."

Dave smirked. "We already did."

J.T. heaved a sigh and headed toward the door. He thanked Jason and Mike, and they left. "Let's call it a night, guys. I'm beat. You can bet Agent Tam is going to have us in the conference room first thing in the morning whether it's a Saturday or not."

Chapter 26

J.T. was surprised that Jade wasn't sitting in the banquet room with a plate of bacon in front of her. He'd sent her a text last night when he returned to the hotel, saying she should call him when she woke up. He hadn't heard a peep from her that morning. He texted her again as he sipped a cup of coffee and munched on a cream cheese–covered bagel.

With the phone on the table, inches away and facing him, he continued his breakfast with one eye on the door. He was sure Jade would walk through any minute. He sighed with relief when his buzzing phone indicated a text had come in. J.T. picked it up and tapped the message icon. The text came from Agent Tam, saying she would be holding the update meeting at nine o'clock in the conference room. She copied the text to everyone in their group. After the last bite of the bagel and a final gulp of coffee, J.T. checked his phone once more for a response from Jade. There wasn't one.

Could she still be sleeping? Maybe she's in the shower.

Anxiety and a gut feeling told him something was off. He took the elevator back to the third floor, walked to room 302, and knocked. There was nothing—not even the sound of the television or the shower running in the background. He pressed his ear to the door—dead silence filled the space on the other side.

She must have gone in early. That's the only explanation.

Logic and common sense told J.T. not to become alarmed. He'd drive to the field office, ride the elevator up to the fourth floor, and find her sitting in the conference room with a cup of coffee cradled between her hands. She'd say she had plenty of sleep and came in early to do research on something.

Yeah, that sounds right. I'm worrying about nothing.

J.T. arrived at the field office at the same time Bruce and Dave did. They parked and walked to the entrance together. Dave glanced back at the parking lot and street.

"Where's Jade?"

"I assume she came in early to do more research on Kent Taylor. I know she was set on finding out where he works so she can make a call to him. Anyway, I didn't see another cruiser in the hotel parking lot when I left."

Dave nodded. "Agent Tam isn't going to be too happy about the videotape results."

"We have a vague idea of Jerry's car, though. I'll call the evidence garage as soon as they open and find out what kind of vehicle he drove."

"It wasn't in the police report?" Bruce asked.

J.T. shrugged. "Not that I noticed."

The men stopped at the vending machine and grabbed a coffee for the meeting.

"Damn it," Dave said as he watched the gray liquid fill his paper cup.

"What's wrong?" J.T. raised his right brow.

"I just remembered Tam always has someone make a pot of coffee for our meetings. I'm sure this swill tastes as awful as it looks."

"Leave it here, then."

"Nah. I'll take it just in case there isn't any upstairs."

The men filled the elevator and rode it up. The doors opened at the fourth floor, and they walked the hallway to the conference room. J.T. checked his watch as he opened the door—the room stood empty.

"Hey, I'm going to run down to the computer lab to see if Jade is in there. I'll be right back. If Tam shows up before I return, tell her where I went."

J.T. took the elevator down to the first floor and rounded the corner at the reception area. Two right turns took him to the hallway where the computer lab was located. With the doorknob grasped in his hand and a quick prayer that she was inside, he pushed the door open to find a darkened room. The sinking feeling in his gut returned— something was terribly wrong. He quickened his pace and went to the reception counter.

"Agent Harper, how may I help you?" the desk attendant, Lisa Drew, asked.

"I'm looking for Agent Monroe. Did you see her come in this morning?"

"I didn't, but hang on, maybe Adrianne did. I'll be right back."

Lisa disappeared through a door that led to a video surveillance room. She was back within a minute with Adrianne Renner at her side.

"Agent Harper, I hear you're looking for Agent Monroe."

"Yes, have you seen her this morning?"

"No, I'm sorry, I haven't."

"Can you check the videos going back a few hours? It's urgent."

"Of course. Come on back with me."

J.T. called Dave's cell as he followed Adrianne. "Dave, something is wrong. Jade is unaccounted for. She didn't answer her room door or my texts this morning. She isn't downstairs, either. I'm heading to the video room behind the main counter at the building's entrance. Adrianne is going to check back a few hours to see if Jade came in. Tell Tam where I'm at."

"You got it. Expect to see us downstairs as soon as she arrives."

J.T. sat by Adrianne's side as she pulled up that morning's camera feed.

"How far back do you want me to go?"

He rubbed his brow in thought. "She said she was tired and needed a decent night's sleep. I can't imagine her coming back too early. Try from six a.m. on."

"Sure, no problem." Adrianne clicked a few buttons and typed in the time frame parameters. The video feed played backward until it reached six a.m. that morning and then began playing forward at a normal speed.

"I can speed it up a bit if you like. I'll pause it if anyone enters the building."

"Yeah, let's try that."

A knock sounded on the door behind them. Lisa came in with Agents Tam, Miller, and Starks at her side.

J.T. looked at his colleagues with concern written across his face. He waved them in.

"What have we got?" Agent Tam asked.

"Nothing yet, boss. Jade seems to have vanished. We've rolled the video feed back to six a.m. Right now it's at six fifty-five, and there's no sign of her."

"Starks and Miller, head to the hotel. Have them pull up their surveillance videos of last night and this morning. We need to see when she entered and when she left again. The room key card panels may be coded to indicate entry and exit time too. Make sure to ask about that. Go now."

"Yes, ma'am." Bruce jerked his head toward Dave. "I'll drive."

Agent Tam pulled up a chair and sat next to J.T. "When was the last time you spoke to Agent Monroe?"

"It was last night in the computer lab. I stopped in just before we left for TaTas. I took a cup of coffee in to her. She said she planned to work for another hour and then go back to the hotel to get a good night's sleep." J.T. shook his head with despair. "She didn't respond to the text I sent last night before I turned in. She didn't come down for breakfast or answer her door when I knocked earlier." J.T. checked the time on the computer screen as he talked. The video was now at seven thirty. "The cruiser she was using wasn't in the hotel lot this morning when I left. Naturally, I assumed she was already here."

"Where are we with the tape?"

Adrianne checked the time stamp. "We're at seven fifty-seven, ma'am, and she hasn't shown up yet."

"The front door is the only place where she, as a guest agent, can enter this building. Am I correct, Adrianne?"

"That's correct, Agent Tam."

"J.T., call Dave and see what they have at the hotel. Tell him to have hotel security open up her room immediately. Adrianne, contact me right away if Jade shows up on the screen."

"Yes, ma'am."

Tam motioned for J.T. to follow while he was talking on the phone with Dave. "Come on. We're going to the hotel too."

Dave waited at the entry for their arrival. Agent Tam and J.T. pulled under the portico five minutes later and parked the cruiser.

"Right this way, ma'am. The last known image of Jade was when she left for the field office yesterday morning with J.T."

"What? You can't be serious."

"Unfortunately, it's true. Bruce is upstairs with hotel security, and they're opening up her room as we speak."

"Lead the way."

J.T. pointed. "Right around this corner." They reached the elevators, and he pressed the button. The bell dinged for the up elevator, and the doors parted. Agent Tam stepped in first, and Dave followed. J.T. entered and pressed the button for the third floor. "This way," he said when they exited the elevator. He led them to room 302, where the door was propped open.

Bruce and the head of security were inside checking the balcony, the closet, the bathroom, and under the bed. He shook his head when they entered. "She isn't here. Her bed doesn't look like it's been touched, either. The closet is full of her clothes, and her cosmetics are still on the bathroom counter. I'm guessing the tapes are correct, ma'am. Jade hasn't been in this room since yesterday morning."

"Bruce, call the downtown PD. Their headquarters are closer to Jordan Taylor's residence than we are. Have a squad go out there and conduct a search under probable cause. Hurry."

Chapter 27

She unlocked the roller door, lifted it three feet, crouched under, and stood up on the other side. She closed it behind her and flipped on the light. Everything remained as she had left it last night. She carried a plastic bag containing a bottle of water and a granola bar. That would tide the agent over for the day. Jordan opened the garbage bag from last night and pulled out the stun gun and syringe. She filled the barrel with a new dose of the drug and dropped both items into her coat pockets. Today, after Jordan tended to Agent Monroe, John Nels would meet his maker. That would leave the best two for last—her final victory. She had to think of a suitable ending for the worst offenders of all.

Jordan rounded the back of the van and clicked the key fob. The door locks popped up, and she cautiously opened the right door, even though Agent Monroe was bound. She didn't need a surprise attack. She peered in and saw Jade sitting against the driver's seat back, facing her.

"Agent Monroe, I see you're awake and doing fine. I'm sure you're thirsty by now." Jordan spoke from the back of the van. "Water and a granola bar will have to do for the time being. I'm kind of in a rush. I don't want to hurt you, so the choice is yours. If you do as I say, you'll remain unharmed. You aren't exactly on my kill list, anyway. Last night I had no other option but to restrain you. I was always a law-abiding citizen until… well, never mind. It isn't your cross to bear. Lie down flat so I can check the zip ties."

Jade rolled to her side and flattened out face down on the steel floor. Jordan climbed up on the bumper and entered the van. The stun gun was gripped in her right hand, ready if needed. She knelt over Jade's back and checked the zip ties, then she gave them an extra pull to snug them tighter. Jade groaned. Her wrists and ankles were already bloodied from the plastic restraints that had dug into her skin.

"Sorry, but I'm doing this for your own good. I'm going to remove the duct tape and rag so you can eat and drink. Go ahead and sit up."

Jade rolled again and pulled herself up into a sitting position. She leaned against the side of the van for support. Jordan removed the duct tape and pulled the rag out of the agent's mouth. Jade sucked in a deep breath and spat out bits of thread from the rag.

"Are you crazy? Do you know what the consequences are for kidnapping a federal agent, not to mention being a serial killer? What did those people do that cost them their lives?"

"Here, have a sip of water. I pulled out your ID last night. Do you mind if I call you Jade?"

"Whatever." Jade jerked her chin. "More water."

Jordan tipped the bottle into Jade's mouth then tore open the wrapper on the granola bar. "Here, eat this. And to answer your question, they're all murderers. I'm righting the wrong, bringing the world back into balance, if you will."

"I wouldn't say killing innocent people brings the world back into balance."

Jordan abruptly stood and glared as she leaned in, only inches from Jade's face. "You don't know me or my story. Those people are far from innocent. The only innocent person in this ongoing nightmare is Emily, and now she's gone."

"And who is Emily?"

"Don't worry about it. I've said too much." With Jordan's arm a blur, and no time to react, Jade was hit again with the stun gun, knocking her senseless. "Sorry, Agent Monroe, but I have places to be and things to do."

She dragged Jade out to the light and sank another dose of Methohexital into her arm. She'd be asleep for hours. Jordan placed several cinder blocks in the back of the van then opened the garage and pulled out. With her car backed in, she transferred Jade to the trunk, jammed the rag back in her mouth, and spread a new strip of duct tape across her lips. She secured the garage door and exited the All-Store facility. She was on her way to John Nels's house. She saw that her cell phone was nearly dead, and a quick stop at home to grab her phone charger would take only a minute.

Alarm bells rang in Jordan's head when two police

squads flew past her as if she was standing still. She closed in on her neighborhood when another whizzed by. Her heart pounded in her chest when two unmarked black cruisers, easily recognized by the government plates and oversized side-mount spotlights, passed her on a residential street. She turned opposite her home, went around the block, and parked along the curb. Between the yards, she had a bird's-eye view of the vehicles in her driveway and spilling out onto the street.

Damn them, now I can't go home. Thank God everything incriminating is out of the house.

Jordan lit a cigarette, shifted the van into drive, and left the neighborhood.

Chapter 28

"Have you reached the residence?" Agent Tam asked Officer Link using the police radio frequency. She and J.T. led in the first cruiser with Bruce and Dave taking up the rear in the second vehicle. The red and blues imbedded in the grille and attached to the visors flashed in each car as they drove.

"Yes, ma'am, and all of the exits are surrounded. We're waiting for Chief Boardman, or you, to give the okay to breach the house."

"Do you have eyes on anyone inside? Can you tell if she's home?"

"Can't tell, ma'am. The curtains are drawn, doors are locked, and there isn't a vehicle in the driveway. The garage has one window with closed blinds on it."

"What's the chief's ETA?"

"He's two miles out."

"And we're double that. Bang on the door, call out her name, and see if she answers. If not, break it down and clear the house. We'll be there in ten minutes."

"Roger that, ma'am."

J.T. picked up his cell and called the evidence garage. He turned toward Agent Tam as he waited. "It doesn't hurt to have more to work with." He raised his hand to indicate the other person had answered. "Hello, this is Agent J.T. Harper with the FBI. What's the status on Jerry Fosco's car?" He clicked over to speakerphone.

"We're nearly done with it, sir. Our findings have been documented with the forensics lab."

"Thank you. I need to know the color, make, and model of that car."

"The vehicle is a 1994 silver Ford Taurus sedan, sir."

"Just what I wanted to hear. Can you transfer me to the tech department, please?"

"Right away, Agent Harper."

J.T. covered his phone's mic with his hand. "The tech department should be able to determine if the car those two people were walking toward at TaTas would fit the description of a 1994 Ford Taurus. After all the circumstantial information we're gathering, I think the case against Jordan Taylor is getting stronger by the minute."

"Agreed." Agent Tam turned in to Jordan's neighborhood and parked along the curb four houses down. "It looks like we have a full crew on-site. I'm guessing that's the chief's sedan parked ahead of us." She killed the engine, then she and J.T. exited the cruiser. Dave and Bruce pulled in right behind them and got out.

The four agents reached the front of the house and saw a number of officers checking the perimeter of the property.

They stepped through the opening where the door had been broken off its hinges and was now propped against the doorframe. Chief Mitch Boardman stood in the living room, talking on his phone while six officers cleared the house. He nodded at the group, said his goodbyes, and hung up. With an outstretched hand, he greeted the FBI agents.

"Mitch, what do we know so far?" Agent Tam asked.

"My guys are clearing the first level then moving on to the attic and basement. So far, it appears the house is empty. That includes the garage, and they haven't found a pair of shoes that matches the tread pattern left on the wall at Mark Fellenz's home."

"Okay, but that doesn't mean she isn't wearing those very shoes. We need the forensic team on-site right away."

He gave her a curious look. "There's no indication that a crime has been committed here, Michelle. Why forensics?"

"It's urgent we find our missing agent. The first thing we need to establish is if we're barking up the right tree or not. Our hunch tells us that Agent Monroe might be in the custody of Jordan Taylor, but we don't know that as a fact. I want forensics to go over this place from top to bottom, fingerprint it, and establish any evidence that would tell us if Agent Monroe has been in this house."

He raked his full head of hair and nodded. "Yeah, understood. Officer Jones, get on the horn and call the forensic team. We need them out here immediately."

"Thank you, Chief. While your men are clearing the house, I'm going out with my agents to start a knock and talk. The neighbors may be able to give us a little insight on Jordan Taylor and possibly a way to get in touch with her husband."

"Absolutely, Agent Tam, and I'll call you as soon as the forensic team arrives."

"J.T., you'll go with me on this side of the street. Bruce and Dave, start on the west side. Hit every house on this block."

"Got it, boss," J.T. said, "and the tech department just confirmed that a 1994 Ford Taurus could be the car on the video of the parking lot at TaTas."

J.T. and Agent Tam crossed the yard to the next house and followed the brick pavers to the front door. They knocked, but nobody answered. They continued on. J.T. paused on the sidewalk, as if in thought.

"Agent Harper, what are you thinking?"

"Maybe I should check in with Jade's family in Wisconsin. I ought to tell SSA Spelling what's going on too."

Agent Tam raised and dropped her shoulders along with an audible sigh. "Give me a second to put this together. We have to make sure we're doing the most urgent things first. That would be to put a BOLO out on Jordan's car and the cruiser and then get her face and description on every news station."

"Even without hard evidence against her?"

"We don't have a choice, Agent Harper. Jade is missing, Jordan is unaccounted for, and the clock is ticking. If we're wrong, I'll make a public apology on television myself."

"Okay, then tell me what you want me to do. I can go back to the field office and put something together for the news stations. I'll make sure to emphasize that Jordan Taylor is currently a person of interest, nothing more. That should cover our butts a little. Before I do that, I think it's imperative to talk to her sister and Spelling. We have to know if anyone has heard from Jade before we make this a TV sensation."

"Go ahead." Tam tipped her head to the left. "I'll be at the next house."

J.T. called SSA Spelling first. He didn't have the numbers of Jade's family or closest friends programmed into his phone. Getting advice from his immediate supervisor could give him additional insight too. He knew he'd be calling his boss at home, and Spelling would likely have to make a call to the Milwaukee field office to retrieve Jade's file. J.T. scrolled through his contact list and tapped the name Phil Spelling.

"Hey, J.T., calling on a Saturday? You must be homesick."

"Boss, we have a problem here in Houston."

Chapter 29

As much as Jordan would have liked to plot and plan a drawn-out ending for John Nels, she didn't have the luxury of time. She sat in the parked van right around the corner from his home and stared out the windshield. Different scenarios bubbled up in her mind.

Unfortunately, John's occupation as a claims analyst wasn't exciting enough to involve instruments she could utilize in his death, but Jordan was sure she could come up with something on the fly.

John was nearing retirement, and so was his wife, Ann. Jordan knew they lived alone and were no match against her, yet she had no beef with the wife. The woman would have to be disabled quickly so Jordan could focus entirely on John. But there was the fact that she'd be able to identify Jordan. Maybe she'd have to die with her husband after all.

Jordan's twisted mind went back to John. He always documented his results in pen and paper on a clipboard, and she was sure she could utilize those tools to her advantage.

Now is as good a time as any. Both cars are in the driveway, and that means I'm going to have to work twice as hard and twice as fast.

With her hand on the doorframe, she stepped down on the running board and exited the van. At the back, she climbed inside and gathered her supplies. The sound of a car engine caught her attention. With the rear doors cracked just enough to peek out, Jordan saw Ann's car back down the driveway and pull out onto the street. She sped away.

Humph. There is a God after all. I wouldn't have felt good about killing that woman.

As soon as the car was out of sight, Jordan made her move. With the stun gun ready and waiting and the backpack slung over her shoulder, she slipped on a pair of gloves as she took the sidewalk to his front door. A blitz attack would get her inside the house quickly. She couldn't have a confrontation with him on the porch, especially on a Saturday when most of the neighbors were home.

She recalled John Nels as a small man, not over five foot seven, if memory served her correctly. Since he was on the pudgy side, it would take a hard push to topple him, but he'd be slow to get up. Once he was down, the advantage would be hers.

Jordan rang the bell frantically, which would cause a rush to answer on his part. He'd already be stirred up by the time he opened the door. The clack of shoes got closer as she held the button in on the doorbell.

The voice on the other side of the door yelled out as he turned the knob. "Hold your horses for crissakes! I'm coming."

The door swung open, and an angry-faced John Nels growled his disdain. In the flash of a second and before he had time to think, Jordan gave him a sharp kick to the gut that sent the man stumbling backward. He hit the wall behind him with a hard thud and slid to the floor. Jordan reached back and slammed the front door then turned the dead bolt latch.

"Remember me, John?"

He coughed as he tried to catch his breath. "No, I have no idea who you are." He scratched at the floor and tried to crawl to safety.

"I'm your judge and jury." She sent a blow to his ribs with her foot then rolled him over and kicked him in the face.

Blood spray dotted the white tile as it squirted from his nose and ran over his lips. He tried to stand, but she kicked his feet out from under him.

"Here's how this is going down, John. You're going to die today, and I'd suggest the sooner the better. Or"—she cocked her head and planted her hands firmly on her hips—"would you rather I take my time and still be here when Ann returns?"

"No, no, please leave her out of this." He wiped his bloody nose with the back of his hand.

"Good, I was hoping you'd agree since I don't have time to spend the entire day with you. Places to go, things to do. You know how it is, right? You see, if I'm still here when Ann returns, I'd have to kill her too. No witness left behind is my motto, and I don't want to hurt your wife since she has no part in this, unlike you. Let's get to it, then, shall we?"

Jordan grabbed the man, zip-tied his hands and legs, then hooked her arm through the crook of his armpit and dragged him to the kitchen, where she propped him on a chair.

"I'm going to be merciful, John, and inject you with a sedative so you don't feel what I'm about to do to you. Consider this your lucky day."

Jordan filled the barrel of the syringe then jammed the needle into John's arm. The drug she pressed under his skin was a lethal dose, but she didn't care. There wasn't time to relish in his suffering. She just wanted him dead. With the ten-foot length of rope she had in the backpack, she tied him to the chair so he wouldn't slide off.

His office was the place she'd search. His clipboard, paperwork, and pens would likely be found on his desk or nearby. She walked the hallway of the sprawling ranch-style home and found his office at the first door on the left. She entered and scanned the room. Plenty of ideas crossed her mind, but she wanted something that indicated his occupation.

"I guess this will have to work, boring as it is."

Back at the kitchen table, Jordan balled up five sheets of inspection paperwork and shoved them as far as she could down his throat, completely blocking his airway. She pulled out his tongue and, with a quick swipe of her pocketknife, sliced it off. She pinched the tongue in the clasp of the clipboard and tossed it on the kitchen table. With a pen in each hand, she jammed them deep into his ears until blood poured out.

"There, that should send a message. You didn't hear the truth and didn't speak it, either. You worked on behalf of all the people that had a part in killing Emily and held nobody responsible. It's time to pay the piper."

Jordan peeked out the window and saw a quiet, unsuspecting neighborhood. She was sure she'd have enough time for the finishing touch. With the backpack in hand, she ran to the van, unlocked the back, and placed a cinder block in the bag. She was back in the house within a minute's time.

"Here goes, John. Have a nice trip to hell." The crushing sound of the block meeting his skull was enough to send a wave of nausea over Jordan for a split second. She almost felt regret. The block dropped to the floor, and she gave him a final look then left. With her head held low, Jordan walked quickly back to the van, climbed in, and sped away.

Chapter 30

"Have you called her family yet?"

"No, you're the first to hear about this, boss. She doesn't answer her phone, she's MIA, and she hasn't shown up on the hotel surveillance tapes since yesterday morning when we drove to the field office together. The cruiser she used wasn't in the hotel parking lot this morning, and she didn't appear anywhere on the field office's tape since she left the building last night."

"Does the car have a tracking device installed on it?"

"Good question. I haven't asked that yet. Hang on." J.T. saw Agent Tam walk out of the second house to his left. He called out to her. "Agent Tam, do the cruisers have tracking systems on them?"

She approached J.T. with concern written across her face. "A tracking device? Not exactly. They have the built-in GPS system that tracks where the driver has been, but you'd have to pull that information right off the car. We can't access that remotely."

"So, that's a no?"

"It's a no unless you're actually in the car."

J.T. got back on his phone. "No, boss, they don't."

"Okay, then you need to get a BOLO out for the cruiser's plate number."

"Already done, sir."

"I'll call you back in five minutes with her contact information, or would you rather I made the call?"

"I'll do it, boss. Somehow I feel responsible. This was her first field assignment, and I should have kept her under my wing."

"Okay, I'll call you right back with her information."

J.T. hung up and faced Agent Tam. "Anything at the second house?"

"Not a lot. The family said they didn't know Jordan and her husband well at all. The occasional wave or a nod, typical neighborly courtesies at best."

"People don't seem to get involved with neighbors much anymore. It's a real shame." J.T.'s phone rang. "Excuse me, ma'am." He walked toward their cruiser to use the hood as a tabletop. "Go ahead, boss. I have my notepad and a pen ready."

With the information for three people in front of him, J.T. had the daunting task of contacting them. He began by calling Amber, the sister Jade had spoken of so fondly. She answered immediately.

"Hello, Amber Monroe speaking."

J.T. heard a questioning tone to her voice and knew there was no reason she'd recognize his number.

"Amber, this is J.T. Harper calling from the FBI."

"*The* J.T. Harper?"

He smiled even though the call was because of an extremely serious issue. "Yes, *the* J.T. Harper. Amber, this is an urgent call. I have to know if you've seen or spoken to Jade."

"What? You can't be serious. What are you trying to say?"

"Jade's gone missing. She hasn't been seen or heard from since last night."

The pause was deafening as J.T. waited for Amber to process what she'd just heard him say. Her lack of a response answered his question.

"Amber?"

"Yes, I'm here, and no, I haven't seen or spoken to Jade since the night before last. Are you sure? This has to be a mistake."

"I wish it was."

"Now what?" Amber's voice cracked, and then the choking, heart-wrenching sobs echoed through the phone line. "I can't deal with another family loss. It's too much."

"Please, Amber, I need your help. Is there any reason I should call your mom?"

"No, I'd be the first person Jade would call if she was back in town. Actually, I'd be the first person to know, then Jack, and then our mom. I haven't missed any calls or texts from her. I always respond. I have to call Jack."

"Is there something more he may know?"

"I don't think so, but I need his moral support right now."

J.T. took a deep breath. "Okay, I'm going to contact the

airport, anyway. I can't think of any reason she'd fly home, but it's something to cross off the list."

"What about the case you guys are working on?"

J.T. heard Amber blow her nose.

"Sorry, but I can't discuss that with you. All I can tell you is we haven't found a connection, but we are checking that angle diligently. Please call me if you hear anything, Amber, and I'll do the same." J.T. hung up and reconvened with Agent Tam, Bruce, and Dave.

Agent Tam led the impromptu meeting at the side of the car. "According to the chief," she said, "there's nothing in the house that leads the PD to think Jade has been inside. Of course, the forensic team will give us a definitive answer on that soon enough. There's also nothing they've seen that incriminates Jordan Taylor of any wrongdoing. There's no sign of Methohexital, syringes, or any drugs whatsoever. There isn't a manifesto, a kill list, or cinder blocks on-site."

"We've been here for over an hour, boss. Where do you think she is?" Bruce asked.

"I have no idea, but it is a Saturday, and she could be anywhere. Did you get useful information from the neighbors across the street?"

"Nah, just what we already know. Jordan keeps to herself, the husband travels a lot for work, and she doesn't have a job."

Dave added, "That would fit in with her ability to ambush a person any time day or night and anywhere."

"Agent Tam." The chief called out from the house. "You'll want to see this."

Tam jerked her head toward the house. "Let's go."

Back inside the residence, the chief led the group to the family room, where a matching set of bookshelves flanked the fireplace.

"There wasn't a reason to go through these books and photo albums, but a quick look by one of the officers brought up something unusual." He pulled out a photo album and flipped open the plastic-covered pages. "I'm assuming this is Jordan Taylor, according to her description. The question is, who is the child in all of these photos? I thought the family only consisted of Jordan and the husband."

Agent Tam held the album in her hand and took a seat on the couch. She turned the pages slowly while she studied the faces in each picture. She tried to make sense of the snapshots in front of her. They began with Jordan and most likely Kent, in a hospital room, proudly holding an infant in their arms. As Agent Tam continued through the pages, she saw a first, second, and third birthday for a little girl sitting in a high chair with Jordan at her side. Photos of Christmases by the tree and snapshots of Easter egg hunts with a happy little girl continued for several pages then abruptly stopped. The rest of the album was empty.

Agent Tam barked out orders. "Get on the horn and find out who this child is. I want to know where she went and why she isn't part of this family any longer."

Chapter 31

With a quick stop at a gas station minimart to pick up supplies, Jordan was back at the storage facility fifteen minutes later. The walls were closing in on her. She felt it and knew she didn't have a lot of time. The cops were going through her home room by room and would likely keep the house under surveillance. There was no turning back. Kent would be home in a day, the cops would question him, and he'd find out everything.

Jordan knew this storage space, a bit larger than a single garage, couldn't be her new residence forever. If she stayed too long, she would be found out by the security detail when they made their occasional trip through the complex. She needed a better idea, and she had to come up with one fast. Kent would be home tomorrow, and the chances of the house being under surveillance were high. He knew nothing of the van, either, but taking the car out again was too much of a risk. As long as Jordan was under a cloud of suspicion, the cops would be on the lookout for her vehicle.

Now what the hell am I going to do? The damn FBI agent is becoming a liability too.

Jade lay in the trunk of the car, and moving her from vehicle to vehicle was risky. Sedating her too often was dangerous as well, and Jordan didn't want the death of an FBI agent on her hands.

I'll hunker down at Jeanie's house for a few days. Nobody even knows she exists. I'll make up something that won't raise suspicion. She's always asking if I want to hang out, anyway.

The sense of closeness Jordan felt toward Jeanie had deteriorated recently, but she had to shelve those feelings temporarily. Finding a place to stay that wasn't on anybody's radar was far more important, but first, she had to tend to Agent Monroe.

Jordan popped the trunk and stared at the woman lying in a fetal position. The agent wasn't moving. Jordan reached in and gave her a nudge. "Hey, wake up."

A parched groan sounded from deep within Jade's throat, and she slowly began to stir. Jordan turned Jade's head and tore the tape off her mouth then removed the rag.

"It sounds like you need a drink of water. I have a sandwich for you too."

Through her cracked voice, Jade spoke. "My head is throbbing. What am I doing in this trunk?"

"You're groggy, and the Methohexital probably gave you a headache. You'll remember everything in a few minutes. Here, sit up." Jordan lifted Jade to an upright position and opened the bottle of water. "Take a sip."

Jade gulped the water. It ran out the sides of her mouth and down her neck. She wasn't fully coherent yet. Jordan wiped Jade's face with a napkin from the stack she'd taken from the minimart.

"We have to talk, Agent Monroe."

"I have to go to the bathroom, and you need to get me out of the trunk. I'm pretty dizzy."

"All I have is a bucket in the corner and these napkins."

Jade nodded. "That'll do, but I need a hand. I'm zip-tied, remember?"

Jordan helped Jade to the bucket and waited while she did her business then walked with her as she shuffled back to the car and leaned against the open trunk.

"Are you going to tell me what the hell this is about?"

"I can't yet. There's still work to do, plus I have to think of something for you."

"I'm a federal agent, and people must be looking for me. You'll never get away with this."

Jordan raked her hands through her hair as she grimaced. "They already are looking for you, and now I can't go home. I have to think."

"Holding me hostage is worsening your position. Just let me go."

"And then what? I've already gone too far. I may as well finish what I've started. The charges against me won't change whether I kill five people or fifty. I'm already serving a life sentence. Being incarcerated isn't going to change that."

"I don't even know what that means."

"You don't need to." She tore off a piece of the sandwich and put it into Jade's mouth. "Eat this. You must be starving."

Jordan walked to the end of the garage and pulled out

her phone. The first call would be to Kent. She had to know his whereabouts and what time he intended to be home tomorrow. After that, she'd call Jeanie. Jordan dialed her husband and waited as the phone rang on his end.

"Jordan, I was about to call you."

"Why? Is something wrong?"

"You sound paranoid, and yes, actually, something is wrong. I'm missing several vials of Methohexital. I wouldn't imagine you'd know anything about that, would you?"

She heard his familiar sneer through the phone lines and was instantly angered. "Are you accusing me of stealing your samples?"

"I am. You know that's a controlled substance and could be lethal if you take too much."

"You want me to take my drugs, and I needed something to help me sleep. When are you coming home?"

"Now that I have to babysit you, I'll be home tomorrow for sure. Stop taking that drug or—"

"Or what, Kent?" she interrupted. "You'll turn me in?"

"Actually, I will, so stay out of trouble. I'll see you tom—"

Jordan cut him off and hung up before he had time to finish his sentence.

Chapter 32

"Agent Tam, a call just came in to dispatch that there's a hit on the BOLO for the cruiser," Chief Boardman said. "Apparently, a security guard at the airport found it parked in the short-term lot."

"Okay, we're on our way. Keep your guys on the house," she yelled back as she rounded up her agents, "and find out who that child is too. Call all the local hospitals and see if Jordan Taylor gave birth at any of them in the last five years." She motioned toward the cars. "Let's go, guys."

The drive from the Taylor home to George Bush Intercontinental Airport would take forty minutes.

"Damn it," Tam said as she hit the steering wheel with her open hand.

J.T. looked across the front seat. "What's wrong, boss?"

"We need the forensic team at the airport, but they're still going through the Taylor house."

"How about the evidence garage's flatbed to haul the car back to the PD? We can give it a quick inspection and send it on its way. By then, forensics should be done at the house."

"Yeah, that should work. Call Dave and tell him to take care of that. Make sure they bring a forensic kit with them."

J.T. made the call as Agent Tam drove.

"Call the airport and have someone from security meet us at the entrance to the short-term lot." She glanced at the clock on the dashboard. "Tell them we'll be there in thirty minutes."

J.T. called airport security, explained the situation then hung up. "They'll be ready and waiting, Agent Tam. Do you want to get Jordan Taylor's profile on the news? If so, it's going to have to be done soon, or we'll miss their prime-time broadcast."

"Let's check out the vehicle first."

They reached the airport, where a white security truck with a light bar on the roof sat waiting. Agent Tam pulled to the curb and got out. J.T. watched as she approached the truck, exchanged a few words, and nodded.

She returned to the cruiser and stuck her head in the window. "The guard is Brian Mays. He's going to lead the way in. I'll tell Dave and Bruce to wait here for the flatbed." She walked to the idling car snugged up behind hers and told the agents what the plan was then returned to her car and climbed into the driver's seat.

Agent Tam followed the truck down five rows, turned right, and drove to the end of the lot. The security guard parked near the chain-link fence and exited his vehicle.

J.T. craned his neck and looked around. He pointed two rows away at a dark sedan. "There's the cruiser."

They followed the security guard on foot to the parked car.

"J.T., take some photographs of the outside and through the windows." Tam jerked her chin toward the guard. "You wouldn't happen to have any gloves, would you?"

"Sorry, ma'am, but no."

J.T. pulled the sleeve of his coat down around his hand and tried the door handles. "Locked. Do you want to break in?"

She nodded the go-ahead, and J.T. walked back to their car, pulled the tire iron from its trunk, and returned to the locked cruiser.

"Stand back," he said. With a forceful tap, he broke the driver's side window. Safety glass spider webbed then spilled out to the ground. J.T. reached in and popped the door locks.

"Get that trunk open before anything. We need to make sure Jade isn't in there."

J.T. reached under the dash and popped the trunk. Tam and J.T. rounded the vehicle and stood at the back bumper. She gave him a nod, and he lifted the trunk lid. They both let out a sigh of relief.

Agent Tam momentarily relaxed her stiff shoulders. "Thank God. Okay, let's get pictures of everything before we start going through the vehicle."

With his cell phone, J.T. snapped a dozen or more images of the car's interior.

"Check this out." He leaned in close and took three pictures of a long blond hair on the driver's seat back. "If I were a betting man, I'd say this hair belongs to Jordan Taylor."

Agent Tam looked in. "I'd have to agree." Her phone rang seconds later. Dave was calling to say the flatbed had arrived. "Okay, lead them in." Agent Tam hung up and addressed J.T. "Snap a few pictures of the trunk too before they show up."

He walked back to the rear of the car and lifted the trunk lid for the second time. "This is interesting."

"What have you got?"

Between his pinched fingers, J.T. dropped what looked to be a mix of sand, gravel, and cement dust into his open palm. "I'd say this is residue from cinder blocks bumping against each other in the trunk."

They turned to see Dave and Bruce directing the flatbed to their location. The two men from the evidence garage exited the truck and approached the cruiser.

"Agents, what have we got?"

"What we've seen on the driver's seat back is a long blond hair that needs to be bagged, and there's a gritty mix of sand and gravel in the trunk. We haven't actually touched anything except the door locks and the trunk latch. I want this car gone over with a fine-toothed comb. Bruce?"

"Yes, ma'am."

"Get forensics on the horn and tell them to collect Jordan Taylor's hair samples from the house. It's a good possibility we're going to have a match. Also, tell the tech department to pull the cruiser's GPS system right away. There aren't any keys in this car, so they're going to have to figure that out. Tell forensics to leave the house now with the hair sample and get to the lab. Go ahead and meet them there."

"You got it, boss."

Agent Tam turned to the waiting men. "Okay, the car is yours. Get it to the evidence garage as soon as you collect those samples." She addressed Brian. "Is this lot monitored with video surveillance?"

"It sure is, ma'am."

"Okay, lead the way. We need to see all the footage between nine o'clock last night and now."

"Follow me."

Agent Tam and J.T. climbed back in their cruiser and followed the white security truck to the employee entrance at the north side of the airport. Through a number of hallways and turns, they finally reached the pulse of the facility—the security department. The enormous room was filled with employees watching monitors for anything that could be considered suspicious.

Brian briefed his immediate supervisor through his walkie-talkie then clicked off. "He should be here in a second, folks."

Agent Tam thanked him, and they waited.

Moments later a man approached them with his hand outstretched. "Bill Harris here. How can we help you agents?"

Tam and J.T. shook his hand and introduced themselves. Tam explained the urgency and said they needed to see the short-term lot videotapes going back twenty-four hours.

"Sure, not a problem. Right this way." Bill Harris led them to the fourth cubical in a row of twelve. "This is Terry Pietry, and he can pull up that footage for you. Terry, go ahead. I'll grab a few extra chairs."

Bill Harris returned moments later with several roller chairs. Terry already had the tape from yesterday ready to roll.

"What are we looking for, ma'am?" Terry asked.

"We're looking for a government-issued black cruiser. According to Brian, it was parked in Row F, all the way to the end near the chain-link fence."

"Sure, I'll pull up that location, and the time?"

Tam looked at J.T., her eyebrows raised in question. "What do you think? Nine o'clock?"

"Let's go with nine thirty."

Tam nodded, and Terry set the time. The tape began with an empty parking spot.

"I can speed it up a bit until the next car enters through the gate. That should make this process go a lot quicker," he said.

"Yeah, let's do that. Time is of the essence."

They focused on the gate area and watched the clock at the bottom right corner of the screen. Three cars entered the lot, but none of them were the black sedan. Time ticked away, and ten o'clock came and went.

"Here we go," J.T. said when the headlights of another car approached the gate. "That's the cruiser."

The overhead lights that shined down on the guard gate confirmed the vehicle was the black sedan.

"Take us back to the camera near the parking spot," Tam said.

Terry clicked the mouse over to camera four. The tape showed brake lights at the last open parking spot. The cruiser pulled in, backed up, and then finally parked. The headlights went out, and the driver's door opened. A tall, large-framed blond woman stepped out of the car, slammed the door behind her, and walked away. The headlights flashed twice, and she headed to the sidewalk.

"Did you see that? She just dropped something into that garbage can," J.T. said as he pointed at the screen. "How far can you follow her?"

"We're pretty much done. The cameras only cover the lot and fifty feet around it. We'd have to pick up her movements with another camera."

"Well, now we know Jade wasn't with her," Tam said. "Can you bring up the tape of the sidewalk area? I want to know if she went into the building or not."

"Yep, just another minute while I switch out cameras. The next tape will take over at the ten fifteen mark."

The tape began rolling with an image of Jordan's back as she walked to the taxi stand and got in line behind a couple with two kids.

"Smart woman, covering her tracks and all," J.T. said. "There she goes. Can you zoom in on the cab number?"

"Not with the sideways angle, but I can get the plates." Terry zoomed in, and J.T. wrote down the license plate number. "All the cabs are through the same company. They're contracted with the airport. Yellow Airport Service is the company name."

Tam and J.T. stood and shook hands with Terry and Bill Harris.

"Thank you for your help," Agent Tam said. "We'll show ourselves out."

Back in the car, J.T. called the cab company, gave them the plate number of the cab, and told them the time in question. He needed to know where that fare was dropped off. The taxi dispatch put J.T. on hold momentarily then came back to the phone with the information.

"That fare was dropped off at the intersection of Fairmont and Clark, sir."

"Thank you." J.T. wrote that down and clicked off. He pulled the location up on his cell phone. "Damn it. That won't tell us anything."

"Why?"

"That intersection is walking distance back to her house. I'm sure she picked that spot deliberately."

Agent Tam's phone in the cup holder rang. She picked it up. "SSA Tam speaking. How may I help you?"

"Michelle, it's Chief Boardman. Things have gone from bad to worse."

"Seriously, how bad can it get? We have a missing federal agent, for crissakes."

"Another murder, that's how bad. I'm texting you the address now."

Chapter 33

"Son of a bitch." Michelle Tam squealed the brakes so hard the seat belts locked up against their chests. She cranked the wheel to the right and skidded to the curb. A billow of smoke from burned rubber filled the air behind the cruiser.

"What the hell is going on?" J.T. jerked his head in her direction and stared.

"That was Chief Boardman. Another murder was just called in, and he's sending me a text with the address." Agent Tam looked out her side mirror and saw Dave running to her car.

He banged on the driver's window. "What happened?"

"Another murder, that's what," Tam said as she lowered the glass. "I want you and Bruce to continue to the forensics lab. We're running out of people that can help. Call the field office and get more agents out here. Have them meet up with you at the downtown PD, update them on everything, and have them wait for the hair sample comparison and the residue analysis from the trunk. We need to know where that cruiser was in the last twenty-four hours. Make sure the tech department gets on that right away. Hang on, Mitch is sending the address." Agent Tam checked her texts and saw the incoming message with an address nearby. "Type this address into your phone, wrap things up at the PD, then meet us there. I'm getting Jordan Taylor's profile on TV today. If the PD wants it, they can get it from every news station that airs in the greater Houston area. Now go."

"You got it, boss."

"J.T., program this address into the car's GPS. It isn't far from here." Agent Tam squealed the tires, hit the lights, and sped away. They'd be at the address in less than ten minutes. "Do you have a copy of Jordan Taylor's driver's license on your phone?"

"Yeah, sure do, boss."

"Okay, start calling every television station. Give them a brief description of her, and tell them she's a person of interest in the recent murders throughout the city and we need her to come in for questioning. Use the reception counter's secondary number at the field office for the hotline number. Call Adrianne and tell her to forward all calls that come in on that line to you, me, Dave, and Bruce. Forward a copy of Jordan's DL to the news stations. Make sure you tell them not to air the entire license on the broadcast. They're only allowed to show her photo and give a verbal description of her height, weight, hair, and eye color. Stress that fact. No pictures of the actual DL. I don't need a lawsuit against the FBI or Houston PD for privacy infringement on somebody that hasn't been officially charged yet."

J.T. pulled up the news channel phone numbers and wrote them in his notepad. He began calling them one by one and forwarded Jordan's driver's license to each of them. "You can use her statistics from the driver's license, but only show the photo. Don't air the actual DL, or you'll be held responsible. Do I make myself clear?"

Each TV station agreed. They were emailed Jordan's information and would break into the currently broadcasted shows. Her photograph and information would hit every news broadcast on every station throughout the rest of the day and evening.

Agent Tam pulled in behind a line of squad cars and the coroner's van. The street was already blocked at the nearest intersections, and two officers busied themselves as they wrapped yellow crime tape around the property's perimeter. Agents Tam and Harper showed their credentials to the officer guarding the front door and crossed into the living room. Inside, stood three officers, two detectives, ME George Craig, and assistant ME Marty Lowrey. They gave a nod when Agent Tam and J.T. approached the kitchen.

"Agents."

"What have we got, George?" Tam asked.

"More brutality, that's for sure. This killer isn't just angry, they're enraged. It's like they've snapped, and all sense of logic and decency has gone right out the window."

J.T. looked around the room and saw only men in blue. "Who called it in?"

"The wife. We thought it best that she went outside. I almost had a heart attack victim on my hands too. I think she's in the back of one of the squads with a female officer."

J.T. pulled an officer to the side. "Has anyone interviewed the wife yet?"

He nodded. "Officer Marsh is doing that in the back of the squad car right now, agent."

J.T. leaned in closely and looked at the clipboard on the table. "Is that what—"

"Yes, that's exactly what it is," George said.

J.T. gave a long, low whistle. "Damn, that woman is really sick." He reached down and scooped cinder block particles off the floor. "We need to see if these granules match the residue from the back of the cruiser. I'm betting they will." He raised his brows at Tam. "Need me in here at the moment? I think I'll go outside and talk to the wife for a bit."

She gave J.T. the go-ahead with a nod then pulled up a chair by the coroner and took notes as he gave his initial assessment of the deceased John Nels.

J.T. approached the officer standing guard at the door. "Which car is Mrs. Nels in?"

The officer pointed at the second squad car in the line of five. "It's that one, sir. Officer Brenda Marsh is with her."

"Thanks." J.T. followed the sidewalk to a squad car with the rear door open. He peered inside and introduced himself to Officer Marsh and to Ann Nels. "May I?" he asked as he pointed at the front seat.

"Sure, go ahead. I can leave if you'd like to speak to Mrs. Nels alone." She began to scoot toward the door.

"No need, Brenda. I'm sure Mrs. Nels would like you to stay. Is that all right, ma'am?"

"Please stay." The distraught woman reached for Brenda's hand and squeezed it tightly. "You've been so kind." Her eyes, swollen and red, showed her anguish.

"Ma'am, I'm sure my questions will be somewhat redundant, but it is necessary that I ask them. I work for the serial crimes unit of the FBI. We're tracking someone that has committed murders similar to your husband's. Has anyone called him lately and threatened him? Has anyone showed up at your door, sent letters or texts to either of you with threats?"

"No, not that I know of. I'm sure John would have told me."

"What was your husband's occupation?"

"He is, I mean was, a claims analyst. He went to accident sites on behalf of the company or person being sued to determine if the claim had any merit or not."

"Do you think your husband had enemies?"

"In that trade, probably, but plenty of claims went through. They weren't all turned down."

"I understand. Where were you today, ma'am?"

"I went to the grocery store, then I dropped a bag of old clothes off at the donation center. I was only gone an hour or so, and I found John that way when I returned home and walked into the kitchen." She buried her face in her hands.

J.T. thought back to the scene. It made sense now that groceries lay scattered about on the kitchen floor. He remembered seeing broken eggs, a few tomatoes, and miscellaneous items at the kitchen entrance as well as one tipped and one standing bag on the table.

Mrs. Nels began crying. "Who could commit such a horrible act on another human being?"

J.T. gave that some thought. Only people who weren't in their right mind could do something that heinous. He wondered what had caused Jordan to snap so severely.

"Ma'am, do you have someone you need to call, any family nearby?"

"Oh no. Patty is going to be devastated when I tell her." Ann Nels put her face in her hands again and sobbed.

"Is Patty your daughter?"

She nodded. "I don't know how to tell her that her dad is gone."

"Ma'am, I can call on your behalf. Maybe it would be best if you spent a few days with Patty. Does she live in the area?"

"Sugar Land."

J.T. looked at Brenda for help.

"It's about forty minutes from here."

"Mrs. Nels, do you have your phone handy?"

"Yes, here it is. Patty's number is the fifth one on my list."

J.T. took the phone and excused himself to talk privately. Giving horrible news to family members was one of the toughest parts of his job. He returned the phone minutes later and told Mrs. Nels that Patty was on her way. J.T. exited the squad car when he saw Dave and Bruce arrive.

"Excuse me, ma'am. I have to talk to these agents. Brenda, you'll stay with her, right?"

"Of course, Agent Harper, not a problem."

J.T. flagged down Dave and Bruce before they entered the house. "What's the word with forensics?"

"Just by visual inspection, they said the hairs were a match. They actually have to do a DNA profile to be certain, which could take up to a week."

"No time for that. We have to find Jade. What about the residue in the trunk?"

"They agree it's from cinder blocks."

"Good enough for me. Do either of you know if Jordan's segment has hit the news stations yet?"

Bruce spoke up. "Don't know, but we haven't received any tip calls."

"Yeah, me, either."

Chapter 34

"Chief, we have a hit on the hospital."

Mitch Boardman excused himself from the call he had made to the precinct and addressed the officer. "What did you find out, Colby?"

Officer Colby pulled out his notepad where he had written down the information. He took a seat at the dining room table of Jordan's house. "Apparently, nearly four years ago, Jordan and Kent Taylor checked into Merciful Savior Hospital, where Jordan delivered a healthy seven-pound-eight-ounce baby girl. They named her Emily Grace Taylor."

"What happened to her?"

"The hospital only has records of her birth, vaccinations, and pediatric wellness exams through age three."

"Did you get the pediatrician's name?"

"Sure did, boss. It's Dr. LuAnn Voight."

"Get on the horn and find out what happened after age three. We need to know where that child is. Keep searching this house for something that may tell us where Jordan

Taylor and Agent Monroe are."

Rachel Fry, the forensic team leader, addressed the chief. "Sir, we haven't found any signs of a struggle or fingerprints belonging to Agent Monroe on-site. There aren't any weapons here, and there's nothing in the attic or basement that would lead us to think somebody had been held against their will. We're spreading ourselves too thin. Half of the team is back at the precinct. I'd like them to check over the cruiser they brought back to the evidence garage as well. Should the rest of us move on to the Nels residence?"

Chief Boardman dug his fists into his pockets and jangled his keys—a sign of angst and frustration on his part. "Yeah, move out. I'll have someone sit on the house." He turned toward Officer Colby. "Colby, I'm stopping at the station to see how it's going with the GPS history. After that, I'm heading to the Nels house. Call me the second you hear from Dr. Voight about Emily Taylor."

"Will do, Chief."

Chapter 35

I watched as Jordan paced back and forth across the garage. She looked to be on the verge of breaking, which could prove dangerous for me.

"We're leaving in a few minutes. You're either getting tied up in the back or you're getting the needle. Decide now."

"I'll sit still. You already have me restrained."

Jordan snickered "Yeah, right. Nice try. I guess you're getting tied up. I don't have much Methohexital left, anyway."

I sighed with exhaustion. The drug was getting the best of me, I was underfed, and I wasn't getting any exercise. My head throbbed most of the time, and I was constantly holding my bladder. I needed this to be over with, and I knew how worried everyone had to be. "Can I see the bottom of your shoes?"

Jordan laughed. "I didn't realize you were into playing games."

"I like games. Humor me."

"Sure, why not?" Jordan lifted her feet to face me. "You have a thing for tread patterns?"

"Actually, I do. Yours look very similar to the pattern on the outside wall at Mark Fellenz's house."

Jordan twisted off the water bottle cap and gave me a sip. "No wonder you're in the FBI. Very observant, Jade. I'll admit, I'm impressed."

I swallowed and wiped my mouth across my shoulder. "I have an idea that could benefit you. It'll show good will."

"Yeah, enlighten me, Agent Monroe. What can *you* do that I care about?"

"Let me call my partner, or at least my sister, to say I'm okay. That will take a lot of the pressure off my colleagues. Otherwise, their instructions will be to shoot to kill once they find us. Turn the locations tab off your phone. I only need a second."

Jordan stood again and paced back and forth through the garage. I hoped she was pondering my suggestion.

"No partner. Who is your sister, and where is she?"

"My sister's name is Amber. She's a sweet kid that lives in Wisconsin, and she can convey the message to everyone else. I hate the thought of her worrying about me."

"Nah, that's not happening. Why would you want to upset your sister any more than she is?"

"It sounds like you care about people."

"Don't try to get in my head, Jade. I'm not stupid. A different name or the call is off the table."

"Okay, my old partner, then, in Wisconsin. He has much tougher skin than Amber. You have to let me do this, Jordan, for your own safety."

She spat at me and sneered. "Actually I don't have to do

a damn thing. You're the one who went snooping in my business, if you recall."

"My job is to uphold law and order."

"So, now you're Olivia Benson?" She laughed and swatted the air then pointed her index finger in my face. "Fine, but this is your only warning. If you say anything other than you're okay, you'll regret it. Tell me the phone number to call and don't get your hopes up. I'm blocking the caller ID."

I rattled off Jack's number, and Jordan tapped the keys. She placed the phone next to my ear, and I listened to the ring. I willed Jack to answer and said a silent prayer that he would, but he didn't. His voicemail picked up, and I left a ten-second message saying I was okay. Disappointment engulfed me, and all hope fell to the pit of my stomach. I needed Jack's familiar voice. He was my savior, my true north. Always was and always would be. I understood why he didn't answer the blocked call. They were usually telemarketers and I never answered blocked calls, either.

"You had your chance, and he didn't pick up, but at least he knows you're fine. It's time to go."

"Where to?"

"To an old friend's house for a while, so get in the van. I need to tie you up."

Chapter 36

Chief Boardman's phone rang right as he reached the precinct. He noticed the name on the screen as he picked up. Officer Colby was calling.

"What did you find out, Colby?"

"The pediatrician finally got back to me. She said Emily Taylor died in a tragic accident on April 23. That was six months to the date of the first killing. Ted Arneson was murdered last Sunday, October 23."

"Did the accident involve cement blocks?"

"You nailed it on the head, boss. Their newly built retaining wall along the side yard collapsed after a solid week of rain. Apparently, the child was playing there, the wall fell, and she was buried under the rubble."

"I wonder where the parents were."

"The doctor didn't have details about that, but she did say she recommended a counselor for Jordan. The therapist's name is Dr. Alan Phelps. I've already left a message with his answering service."

"Good work, Colby. Now we know the reason Jordan went

off the deep end. What we don't know is what spurred that six-month trigger. Keep digging and keep me posted. The news segments should be going out with Jordan's name and face. It won't be long before this nightmare is over and she's in custody. I'll call the agents and let them know our latest findings."

Chief Boardman hung up and turned in to the precinct's parking garage. The first spot nearest the door had his name on a placard bolted to the wall. He killed the engine and went inside then headed downstairs to the tech department. The best way to locate Agent Monroe would be to see where the cruiser had been in the last twenty-four hours.

He entered the well-lit room and approached Mike Walters. "What's the word, Mike?"

"Hey, boss. I'm hooking up the cruiser's GPS device to our system so I can open its history. I should have it ready to go in about fifteen minutes."

"Call my cell the minute you know something."

"Will do, sir."

Mitch tapped the green telephone icon next to Agent Tam's name, and she picked up immediately. "Michelle, I left the precinct a few minutes ago, and I'm heading to the Nels house. I have new information. Are you still there?"

"Yeah, I'm here. Give me just a second, I'm walking outside. This scene is as horrific as the others, Mitch."

"I'm sure it is. I'll update you in a few minutes. I'm almost there." The chief clicked off and turned onto Pilgrim Avenue moments later. He saw Agent Tam standing on the sidewalk with Dave, Bruce, and J.T. He pulled his cruiser over to the curb and exited the vehicle.

"I'm glad you're all together. I have some important news. First off, the tech department is pulling up the history on the cruiser's GPS system. Mike should be calling any minute."

Agent Tam breathed a sigh of relief. "Good, maybe we'll find Jade before the day is done. Anything else?"

"There's plenty more. Six months ago last Sunday, Jordan Taylor's three-year-old daughter was crushed to death by a falling retaining wall. The pictures in the album were of her daughter, Emily. Of course, the photos stopped after the child died. Everyone that has fallen victim at Jordan's hands was likely part of the crew that surveyed, designed, and built that wall."

"And that's why a cinder block or some form of cement was at every scene. Why dismember the people, and what about the 9-1-1 operator, though? What was Jordan's beef with her?" J.T. asked.

"We haven't found that out yet, but we will. We're closing in on Jordan, and she'll be in custody soon."

"I wonder what brought on the killings now. Six months have gone by."

"Not sure, Agent Sparks, but something triggered her rage. We have a call out to the therapist she was seeing. Maybe Dr. Phelps can shed some light," Chief Boardman said.

J.T.'s phone rang in his pocket. "Excuse me." He took a few steps farther down the sidewalk and answered. "Hello, Agent Harper here."

"J.T., it's Amber Monroe, Jade's sister. She called. Jade is okay!"

"What in the world are you talking about? What do you mean Jade called? When?"

"She called Jack Steele, her old partner, probably because she had his number memorized. He didn't pick up, so she left a short message that said she was okay. Jack didn't have your number, so he called me."

"How long ago did that call come in?"

"Less than an hour ago, according to Jack. I'm so relieved, Agent Harper. Do you have any leads?"

"We're getting there, Amber. I need Detective Steele's number. I have to speak with him now."

Amber rattled off the number, and J.T. thanked her and hung up. He called Jack immediately to hear firsthand what was on Jade's voicemail message.

"Hello, Jack Steele speaking."

"Detective Steele, it's Agent Harper. I know we've never been formally introduced, but let's save that for another time. Amber Monroe just called and said Jade left a message on your phone. I need the details."

"I'm still kicking myself for not picking up. The message was short, only seconds long. One brief sentence saying she was okay. The call disconnected right after those words."

"Shit. Nothing else?"

"Not a thing. The call came in forty-seven minutes ago."

"What about a number?"

Jack chuckled. "You're FBI. You know better."

"Yeah, wishful thinking, that's all. The last time I saw Jade, she was working in the field office computer lab. She was trying to find out more about our suspect's husband. I took her a coffee, and she said she was going to work for another hour then go back to the hotel and get a good night's sleep. Nobody has seen her since. There isn't even footage of her entering the hotel that night. Is there anything else you can tell me?"

Jack's sigh was audible through the phone line. "That sounds like Jade."

"Meaning?"

"It means you don't know her quite well enough. Don't get me wrong. She's an ace detective, always has been. Jade has a renegade streak, likely learned by watching her old man over the years. Not that she goes off halfcocked, she's very thorough, but not cautious enough about her own well-being. She's gone rogue several times in the past."

"Great. So it wasn't like our suspect came after her. More the opposite?"

"Sorry, but likely. Jade either had an epiphany or found something she needed to check out. That's usually what sets her in motion."

"We don't do things like that in the FBI."

"We don't, either, Agent Harper. Jade's saving grace is she always solves the case and lands on her feet, even when putting her own life at risk. If I hear anything else, I'll contact you directly now that I have your number."

"Thanks, Jack, and I'll keep you posted too." J.T. clicked off the call and yelled out to the others. "Jade called her old partner just an hour ago. She said she's okay, now let's find her!"

The chief's phone rang. He swiped the screen from left

to right and answered. "I'm putting you on speakerphone, Colby. What do you have?"

"Hey, boss. I just spoke with the therapist, Dr. Phelps. He told me that Jordan has canceled her last two appointments and is on strong medications. He wouldn't go into detail about her condition and cited doctor-patient confidentiality."

"Yeah, yeah, I guess it isn't important enough to issue a warrant, and we don't have that kind of time, anyway. We already know she's off her rocker and likely off her meds. Good work, Colby. Keep us posted."

"Now we just need to hear from the tech department," Bruce said. "Why haven't any tip line calls come in yet? The segment on Jordan has to have aired by now."

Tam jerked her chin at Bruce. "Call Adrianne and find out what's going on. Don't people watch TV during the day?"

Chapter 37

"We're getting close, Jade. We'll be there in a few minutes." Jordan turned right onto Lincoln Street and went several blocks. "You're going to stay here while I go inside. As soon as it gets dark, I'll pull the van into the garage."

Jordan looked over her shoulder at the agent gagged with tape and tied to the floor with rope. Jordan had removed the zip ties on Jade's wrists and replaced them with her own handcuffs. The agent's wrists, raw from the plastic restraints digging into her skin, were given a temporary rest. The looser handcuffs allowed room to weave the rope through and secure each side to the bolts in the van. Jade lay flat on the floor, splayed out and unable to move left or right. Jordan glanced back at Jade again and saw her looking out the tinted side window.

"Enjoying the view? It's been a few days since you saw the sky and trees."

Jade mumbled inaudible words through the gag and stared out the window.

Jordan slowed and pulled over to the curb then killed the

engine. With her arm stretched over the bench seat, she spoke to Jade. "It's going to be a few hours. I can give you the needle if you want to sleep for a while. The time will go faster."

Jade shook her head.

"Suit yourself. I'll be back later."

Jordan pulled up the hood on her black sweatshirt and opened the driver's side door. She scanned her surroundings then stepped down off the running board. The click of the fob and double beep told her the van's doors were locked. She dropped the keys in her pocket and headed up the sidewalk.

"Damn it, I forgot my backpack." She returned to the van and unlocked the back doors. "It's just me again. I forgot something." She reached in and grabbed the black bag, slammed the doors at her back, and locked the vehicle for the second time.

Jordan parked two blocks from Jeanie's house. She didn't want to hear any questions about the van. She rang the bell and waited on the stoop. Boozer jumped to the windowsill and scratched at the already mangled curtains.

Jordan scowled at the cat through the glass. "I hate you."

Jeanie's yell and the cat's hiss and hunched back told Jordan the animal had been busted for shredding the curtains again. It disappeared from view as footsteps got louder. The door swung open.

A surprised expression crossed Jeanie's face. "Jordan, I wasn't expecting you this early." She glanced out to the driveway. "Where's your car, and why are you dressed that way?"

Jordan stepped around Jeanie without answering the

question. "Who are you, the fashion police? Would you rather I leave?"

"Don't be ridiculous. Come in. It's been way too long. You're always in the middle of something when I call."

Jordan smirked. "You have no idea."

"What's with the backpack?"

"Girl stuff, that's all." Jordan hung the bag over the back of a kitchen chair and took a seat.

Jeanie sat across the table, facing her. "So, what do you want to do this afternoon? Have you been to the mall lately? We can start our Christmas shopping early."

Being out in public wasn't the smartest idea. And Christmas shopping? Jordan didn't want to think about her first Christmas without Emily. "Nah, I'm not in the mood to shop." She needed to hunker down until Kent returned tomorrow. "Let's have coffee and catch up."

"Ooh, that sounds juicy. Want to go out or stay in?"

"Let's stay in. I've been a little on edge lately. I'm looking forward to Kent coming home in the morning."

Jeanie scooped coffee grounds into the filter, poured water in the reservoir, and hit the green button. "Oh, I thought—"

"You thought what?"

"Nothing, I misspoke."

"No you didn't. Finish your sentence."

Jeanie looked nervous. "Jordan, relax. You really are edgy, almost to the point of being combative."

"Am I? I just wanted to hear what you were going to say. It was about Kent, wasn't it?"

"Kent? Of course not. Why would you even suggest that? Come on. Let's sit in the living room and catch up. The coffee is ready."

Jeanie poured two cups, and with one in each hand, she took them to the living room and set them on the coffee table. Jordan followed closely at her back.

"I'll turn off the boob tube so we can visit without that distracting drone." Jeanie reached for the remote that sat on the entertainment center. She stopped in her tracks and stared at the television screen.

"What's wrong?" Jordan asked as she sat on the couch. Something was off, and Jeanie's body blocked her view. She did hear the words *breaking news,* though.

"Jordan?" Jeanie turned to face the woman that stared at her from across the room. Fear clouded her eyes. "Why are you on TV?"

In two strides, Jordan was at Jeanie's throat and had her in a choke hold. She squeezed hard, cutting off Jeanie's breathing. The woman fell limp under the pressure of Jordan's forearm against her neck and slumped to the floor.

The breaking news segment continued. Jordan stared at her own face looking back at her. The anchorman continued with the segment, saying Jordan Taylor was a person of interest in a rash of killings throughout the greater Houston area.

Jordan grabbed her backpack and unzipped the outer pocket. A quick zap with the stun gun would silence Jeanie temporarily until she formulated a plan. She pushed Jeanie's hair to the side and exposed her neck. With the red button held down, Jordan watched as the electric charges bounced back and forth between the posts and burned eraser-sized marks into Jeanie's skin.

Jordan dropped to the chair—this wasn't the way she imagined the evening playing out. She had much better intentions in mind.

Damn television, damn anchorman, damn Jade Monroe. Why can't everyone leave me the hell alone?

The anger building inside Jordan sent her into a near-hysterical rage. She felt like a caged animal, and everyone's interferences were making her task more difficult. They would pay dearly. In her rage, she balled her hand into a fist and pummeled Jeanie's face. The unconscious woman lay on the floor with blood running down the sides of her cheeks.

"Where are your damn car keys?" Jordan screeched as she pressed her temples. The thick vein centered on her forehead bulged with a deep shade of blue. Her darting eyes frantically searched the kitchen countertop and the drawers for the car keys. She turned the corner to the mudroom. A board nailed to the wall held five coat hooks—two had Jeanie's jackets slung over them. Jordan checked the pockets in the first jacket and felt the cold metal set of keys. "It's about damn time." She yanked them out and opened the door that led into the garage then slapped the light switch and hit the button on the wall to lift the overhead door.

Jordan looked over her right shoulder as she backed Jeanie's car out of the garage and parked it alongside the driveway. With the door slammed at her back, she jogged the two blocks to the van and climbed in. She turned the key in the ignition and shifted into drive, then she pulled ahead and entered the garage. Once out of the driver's seat, Jordan hit the wall switch to close the overhead then stormed to the back of the van. She flung the doors open and glared at Jade.

"You stupid bitch and your FBI friends couldn't leave well enough alone. I just saw my own face on TV, thanks to you. And now?" Jordan laughed bitterly. "Now you're going to be in a world of hurt once I get your ass inside the house."

She climbed up on the bumper and entered the back of the van.

Chapter 38

"Shut the hell up, or I'll put that tape back on your mouth. I don't want to hear a peep coming from you."

I cried out in pain as my arms were wrenched unnaturally behind my back. Jordan removed the handcuffs and zip-tied my wrists together for the umpteenth time, then she shoved me to the back doors of the van and told me to get out. With a giant misstep and legs that were tied together, I fell to my knees on the concrete garage floor.

"Get up and go in the house," she said as she pulled the last two cinder blocks out of the van and placed them against the garage wall.

I groaned with aching kneecaps. "Where are we, and what are you going to do with those blocks?"

"It's not your concern, now stand up."

"How am I supposed to get up those steps with my legs shackled?"

"You have thirty seconds to figure it out."

I scooted up each step on my butt until I reached the top, then I stood with my back against the door and turned the knob. The door swung open, and I toppled against the wall in what looked to be a mudroom and fell to the floor.

Jordan grabbed the zip ties between my legs and dragged me through the mudroom and kitchen then into the living room where I saw an unconscious woman. Blood glistened in her hair and stained the tile beneath her head.

"Oh my God," I cried out.

"God's busy doing other things. He isn't going to help you just like he didn't help Emily."

"You still haven't told me who Emily is," I snarled. My eyes darted back and forth as I checked my surroundings. I tried to pick out something, anything that would help me get myself and this unknown woman out of our predicament. I had no idea who she was or whether she was alive. "Jordan, I know people that can help you with your demons."

She reached down and grabbed a fistful of my hair and gave it a hard yank. "You don't know shit. Now shut up."

She delivered a swift kick to my side and knocked the wind out of me. I groaned and rolled into a fetal position to protect my body. A guttural sound came from the woman behind me—she was still alive. I turned to face her. A quick assessment told me her nose was likely broken. She'd be lucky if that was the extent of it. I looked across the room and saw the television playing. With my tear-blurred eyes, I stared at the screen and recognized the Channel 58 news anchor. I remembered the local news played the latest highlights at five o'clock, and that segment was all about Jordan. Now I knew what had set her off. I was thankful and fearful at the same time.

"Hey, over here," I whispered when Jordan disappeared into the kitchen. "Turn this way. Look at me."

The woman moaned in pain. Her face, covered in blood, was horrific, but her eyes widened in what looked like hope when she saw me.

"How badly are you hurt?"

She responded in a raspy whisper, "I don't know, but it's hard to breathe."

I nodded. "Your nose is probably broken. Consider yourself lucky if that's the worst of it. I'm an FBI agent. I have to find a way to get us out of here. Is this your house?"

She nodded as she tried to get up.

I shook my head. "Stay down. Don't give her a reason to go after you again." I heard Jordan approaching. "Shhh, close your eyes and let me handle this."

Chapter 39

Bruce handed his phone to Agent Tam. "Ma'am, Adrianne needs to talk to you."

"Excuse me, folks." Michelle Tam leaned against the cruiser and answered. "Adrianne, what have you got? Are calls coming in?"

"Yes, ma'am, but they're from Jordan's neighbors, the same people we've already interviewed."

"Seriously?" Tam let out a deep sigh. "Any others?"

"No, ma'am, but the local news at five just began. People tend to watch that as they're making dinner. Hold for one second. Another call is coming in."

Agent Tam waited and listened to elevator music for nearly a minute.

"I'm back, ma'am. That was Mike Walters from the tech department. Apparently he called Bruce's phone, but it went directly to voicemail."

"Because we're talking on it. What did he say?"

"He has the GPS history ready. He asked for you or Chief Boardman to call him right away."

"Thanks, Adrianne." Agent Tam clicked off and yelled out to the group, "Mike has the cruiser's GPS history ready. Give him a call, Mitch. It's time to find Jade."

The group congregated at the cruiser while Chief Boardman had Mike on speakerphone.

"Mike, what have you got?"

"This is the history going back twenty-four hours, boss. The car was stationary at the field office until eight forty p.m. At nine o'clock it stopped a few doors down from Jordan Taylor's address."

J.T. shook his head. "Jack said she probably wanted to check out something. Apparently she felt the need to park away from the house so she wouldn't alert Jordan."

"As in sneaking around?" Agent Tam asked.

J.T. shrugged. "It would seem so, ma'am."

"Then where, Mike?"

It was at your location for less than a half hour then drove another twenty minutes and stopped. I pulled up the address, and it's an All-Store storage facility."

"Bingo," Tam said. "Saddle up, people, we're heading out. Is that the last stop before the airport?"

"It is, ma'am."

"Great work, Mike. Text that address to our phones and call the storage facility to make sure someone is on-site to allow us through. We need the number of her unit and any videotapes they may have. I want them up and ready for us to look at."

"I'm on it, ma'am."

"Okay, let's roll!"

Chief Boardman called out to the remaining officers to secure the house and keep it under surveillance. The agents climbed in their cars and peeled out, en route to the All-Store facility with the chief, in his cruiser, leading the way.

With heavy traffic ahead, the officers engaged their lights and sirens. They didn't have time to waste. The three cruisers arrived at the facility twenty minutes later and squealed to a stop at the gate. Agent Tam slammed the shifter into park and exited the vehicle. She approached the guard shack and spoke to the person inside the small booth. She asked for Jordan Taylor's unit number. The guard checked the log of rental units.

"Nobody under that name has a unit here, ma'am. Are you sure you're at the right facility?"

"Yes, I'm sure, damn it. She's a tall blond woman that drives a 2009 dark blue Accord."

"Yeah, okay. That's Angela Gates." He checked the log again. "She's in Row C at the far end, unit 66."

"Is this facility monitored with video?"

"Sure is."

"Good. I want the tape for the last twenty-four hours up and ready before we leave this facility. Do you have keys for each unit?"

"Nope. Everyone secures their space with their own lock and key."

"Good enough. If it's locked, you're going to hear a gunshot. If there's anyone here other than us, I want them ushered out for their own safety. Close this place up and don't let anybody in until we're done here. Understand?"

"Yes, ma'am." He lifted the gate, and Agent Tam returned to the car. "Follow me," she yelled out as she climbed in the cruiser and sped down Row C.

They reached the last unit in that row, private and snugged in against the chain-link fence. The agents and Chief Boardman exited their cars and approached the overhead roller door. J.T. put his ear against the metal and held up his hand. Everyone fell silent as he listened. He shook his head.

"Nothing, there's no sound inside." He tugged on the handle and the lock. They weren't budging. He looked from face to face. Agent Tam nodded the go-ahead. "Okay, back away." He pulled out his sidearm, shielded his face with his forearm, and took aim. With one shot, he blew the padlock off the latch. J.T. grabbed the handle and lifted the roller door.

They found the blue Accord parked inside.

"No wonder the BOLO hasn't hit. The car has been hidden away in this storage unit. Get that trunk popped," Boardman yelled out.

With his arm stretched to the latch under the dash, J.T. gave it a pull, and the trunk lid opened.

Dave looked in and let out a relieved sigh. "It's empty."

Tam jerked her chin at Bruce. "Go back to the guard shack and have him pull up the surveillance tape. She's using another vehicle, and I want to know what it is right now."

Bruce jumped in the cruiser and sped back to the guard shack. He returned fifteen minutes later with the necessary information written on a sheet of paper.

"She's driving a white van, boss. The footage was grainy, but the grille emblem could be the Chevy logo. It had limousine tinted side windows too."

"Okay. Did you get the plate number?"

"No plate on the front, and I couldn't see below the back doors."

Tam growled under her breath. "All right, I'll look at the video myself later. Right now I want everything in this garage gone over. We need to know if Agent Monroe has been here or not."

"Boss, check this out," Dave said. "There's bloodstained zip ties and a makeshift toilet back here in the corner. Jordan must have camped here overnight."

Boardman piped up. "Those zip ties are probably our best evidence of Jade being here." He poked his head into a garbage bag wedged in the corner. "Empty water bottles, granola bar wrappers, yep, I'd say this is where they hunkered down." He huffed and planted his hands on his hips. "I believe I just found our murder weapons." He tipped his head to the right. "There are several dozen broken cinder blocks stacked against this back wall."

"Take pictures of everything, Dave, especially those blocks, and get a count on them too," Tam said.

J.T. paced the garage and scratched his two-day stubble. "Okay, they're in a white van, and Jordan could be using it as their temporary living quarters. Damn it. She could be anywhere. Hasn't anybody found the husband yet?"

Nobody spoke up.

"She could be long gone if she caught wind of the news broadcasts," Tam said. "Chief, what's your gut telling you?"

"It's telling me to check that video myself and see if there's any identifying features on that vehicle, then we need to get a BOLO out for it. I don't care if every white van in the state is pulled over and searched. Let's put that info on the digital freeway signs too. After that, we have to update the news stations to include a white van with the information about her."

"Okay, people, keep searching this unit. Chief Boardman and I are going to the guard shack to review that tape."

"Hold up." J.T. knelt on the floor at the right rear side of the car. "Check this out."

Tam turned. "What do you have, Agent Harper?" The group rounded the car and peered over J.T.'s shoulder.

Scratched into the cement floor with what looked to be smears of blood mixed in were the letters JM.

"JM, Jade Monroe." Tam pointed several inches to the right. "See that small gravel stone with blood on it? That's probably what she used to etch her initials with. The blood smears make sense if those zip ties in the corner were around her wrists at the time. They were likely cutting into her skin." Tam pushed off her knees and stood. "There's biological evidence here, meaning we need forensics on-site." She barked out orders before she and Boardman left for the guard shack. "Call everybody that's available from the forensic team. We need them out here now. Get a picture of those initials too. This is turning into a shit storm faster than we can keep up."

Thirty minutes later, a group of officers, agents, and forensic specialists were gathered at the storage garage. The BOLO had been issued to law enforcement statewide, and the digital freeway signs flashed the alert to watch for a white van with black-tinted side windows.

Chapter 40

I watched as Jordan turned up the television and took a seat on the couch ten feet to my left.

"What's the plan, Jordan? Who is the woman lying here, and why did you attack her?"

"I have my reasons, none of which is any of your concern."

"She could die. She needs medical help."

"Nah, she isn't going to die until I say so. The time isn't right yet but probably tomorrow."

I scooted closer to the woman. Her back faced Jordan, and she opened her eyes as if to tell me she was still conscious.

I gave her a thin smile then addressed Jordan again. "What's her name? How do you know her?"

"That's Jeanie, my oldest and dearest friend. We've known each other since high school."

"I don't understand why you attacked her, then."

Jordan crossed the room and knelt at my side. "Here's the deal, Agent Monroe. Shut the hell up! If I want to play the twenty questions game with you, I'll let you know. Until then, it isn't in your best interest to get on my nerves. Got it?"

I nodded. Jordan pushed me aside and sat between us, blocking my view of the injured woman.

"Wake up."

Jeanie remained motionless. Jordan stood and rounded the corner to the kitchen. I heard the sound of cabinet doors banging and then water running.

"How are you holding up?" I whispered.

The injured woman was the only glimmer of hope I had since she wasn't tied up, but I couldn't ask her to put herself in more danger. She had already sustained serious blows to the face, plus she was no match for Jordan, who outweighed her by fifty pounds.

Jeanie gave me a slight nod then closed her eyes—Jordan was returning.

I rolled onto my back so I could keep my eye on Jordan. She stepped over me with a glass of water in her hand and knelt in front of Jeanie.

"Wake up." She waited a few seconds and then stood and threw the glass of water in Jeanie's face.

The woman gasped and cried out, as if in shock.

"That's what I thought, faking it. Ice water is a little startling, isn't it?"

Jordan slammed the glass to the floor, and it shattered only inches from both of our faces. She turned toward the TV when more breaking news came on the local station.

"Now what?"

Glass shards lay within reach of Jeanie, and her hands were free. This was my only chance to make a move while Jordan was preoccupied. I tipped my head to get Jeanie's attention. She followed my eyes to a large piece of glass only five inches away. I nodded and rolled to my side. She slipped the piece of glass between my clasped hands.

Jordan leaned forward. Her elbows rested on her knees, and her face was propped between her open palms. Her attention was focused on the television. The anchorman spoke about the latest developments in the case.

"The FBI and local PD have shared new developments in the Jordan Taylor investigation. Authorities believe the woman is driving a white van with blacked-out side windows. Do not approach any vehicle fitting this description. The woman may be armed and dangerous, and the FBI has reason to believe she is engaged in a hostage situation. Law enforcement is reaching out to the public. Please call the tip line at the bottom of the screen if you see anyone fitting Jordan Taylor's or this vehicle's description."

She turned toward me and glared. "This has escalated to a hostage situation because of you."

I knew it was coming and braced for it. She crossed the gap between us in two strides, and I was on the receiving end of a hard strike to the ribs. I tried to pull my knees to my chest to protect my body, but she was too fast. I grunted in pain as she gave me a second hit.

"I've had enough. It's time to release a little anxiety." Jordan opened her backpack and pulled out a length of rolled paracord and the duct tape.

This wasn't going to turn out well, and I had to hurry. My hands, hidden from view, worked diligently to cut through the zip ties securing my wrists. I felt the slippery, sticky wetness of blood as I sawed through the plastic cuff with the shard of glass. I knew I was cutting into my own flesh with every attempt, but I continued on.

Jordan kicked the remaining slivers of glass, and they skidded across the floor. She grabbed a chair from the kitchen and placed it next to Jeanie then leaned over her and snickered. "Ready?" She yanked the woman up by her hair and pushed her down on the chair.

Jeanie flailed and tried to break Jordan's grip, but it was useless. She was punched in the side of the head and fell silent.

I yelled out as a diversion, "Jordan, leave her alone. Focus on me. I'm the one you're angry with."

"I'm angry with everyone. Don't worry. You'll get your turn."

Jordan grabbed the red paracord and wrapped Jeanie tightly in the chair.

"You're lucky I'm holding off until tomorrow to kill you, or I'd be wrapping this entire roll of tape around your head right now."

I watched as Jordan tore off a six-inch strip of duct tape and placed it over Jeanie's mouth. If Jeanie's nose was actually broken, her airways were already constricted. I didn't have a lot of time.

With the job complete and Jeanie restrained, Jordan took a seat and flipped the TV stations. She leaned to the side and pulled the ringing phone out of her back pocket and checked the screen. She stood and grinned before leaving the room. "Don't go anywhere, guys."

This was my chance. I felt the plastic ties snap as I pulled my hands in opposite directions. I had no idea how many seconds or minutes I had left before she would return. I needed to hurry. With the bloody piece of glass, I sawed at the ties around my ankles, willing them to break loose. I heard Jordan talking from a room down the hall as I cut through the plastic. I broke free of the final restraints that held me back and jumped to my feet. I heard her say goodbye, then the sound of footsteps got closer. I had two seconds—maybe three—to find something to disable her with. I grabbed the first thing I saw, a decorative wooden statue, and swung. She teetered, probably with surprise more than pain. I saw her lunge, then I felt my head bounce off the floor.

Chapter 41

Jordan tossed the drugged and unconscious agent into the back of the van. Jade Monroe had proven to be too much trouble to keep around. She was a distraction that served no purpose, and Jordan needed her focus to be on the last two people on her list. After that, she didn't care what happened.

The sun had dipped beneath the horizon a half hour earlier, and she was almost at her destination. Sheldon Lake State Park closed at five o'clock daily, and there were far fewer visitors during the cooler season. She was sure she'd have the park all to herself. Jordan turned in and saw the heavy chain secured across the driveway—a good sign. The park was buttoned up for the night. She shifted into Park, got out and lowered the chain then returned to the van and drove through. Once she cleared the chain, she got out and secured it across the driveway again. She continued on. Jordan knew this park well and the vast wetlands within it. Nobody would come across Agent Monroe anytime soon or even think to look for her there.

The walking paths were wide enough for vehicles to use and zigzagged throughout the enormous park. Jordan followed the main road that passed the environmental learning center then turned off onto a path that led deeper in. She continued beyond the picnic tables and fishing piers then entered areas that the public seldom saw.

She killed the engine, got out, and opened the van's back doors. Agent Monroe lay passed out on the floor and would likely be asleep until morning. Jordan had given her the last dose of Methohexital she had. With the flashlight in one hand and the agent flung over her shoulder, Jordan followed a deer trail until the soggy ground made the hike too difficult. She dropped Jade on the mucky surface.

"There," she said as she shined the flashlight toward the ground. The wetland's tall grasses and reeds concealed Agent Monroe, and she was well hidden within them. "I don't even want to know what kind of critters are going to be checking you out tonight." Jordan gave the agent a final look before walking away. She was sure that would be the last time she'd cross paths with Jade Monroe.

Chapter 42

The agents sat in the command center at the downtown police department with the chief and a squad of fifteen officers and detectives. All of the tip line calls that came into the FBI field office had been diverted to the police station, where they could all work together as a team. So far, at six o'clock, none of the calls had resulted in viable leads.

The command center consisted of a long table in the middle of the room and a bank of telephone and computer stations against the east wall. A large map of Texas hung on the south wall, and another map, the same size, but of Houston, hung on the west wall.

Dave, Bruce, and two detectives tapped computer keys, looking for something that could lead them one step closer to finding where Jordan and Jade might be. J.T. and five officers stationed themselves at the phones. Tips were pouring in, and every one of them had to be checked out.

Sheriff's department deputies, along with the state patrol, watched the interstates, state highways, and country roads. Every white van, whether it was registered in Texas or somewhere else, was pulled over and the occupants questioned.

"Tomorrow is day two, and we don't have a damn thing." J.T. was beside himself with worry. "We've found where they've been, we just don't know where they are. The freeway signs are doing their job, but Texas has 1,400 white vans registered in the state, and there are hundreds more passing through."

Dave pulled up every pharmaceutical company in the state and printed out the name, location, and phone numbers. There were forty-seven, and every one was closed over the weekend. They had no idea where Kent Taylor worked or if he even worked for a company that was based in Texas. No phone or tax records for Jordan or Kent had been found in the house during the search that morning.

"The IRS could help us. They can pull up Kent Taylor's latest tax return and tell us where he works."

Agent Tam chimed in. "That's true, Bruce, but only with a court order and certainly not on a weekend. No matter what, that would still take time that we don't have."

J.T. hung up the phone. "An elderly lady"—he looked at his notes—"Edith Smart, who lives on Lincoln Street, just called. She said she watched the news and recalls seeing a white van parked across the street earlier today."

"Anything else?" Chief Boardman asked.

"Only that it was there for about a half hour, then it was gone. She said it had a missing hubcap on the back driver's side. Where's Lincoln Street from here?"

One of the detectives stood and jabbed his finger at a

spot on the Houston map. "Right here." A red push pin indicated where the police department was located.

"How far is that, ten minutes away?"

The detective nodded. "Yeah, about that."

Tam looked at Boardman. "Did the video at the storage facility show a missing hubcap?"

"I didn't notice. I was too busy trying to figure out the van's make and model."

"Bruce, do you recall seeing a missing hubcap?"

"Can't say I do, boss, but I'll call the storage facility and have the guard take a closer look at the footage."

"Yeah, get on that." Tam tipped her head toward J.T. "Go ahead and get the old woman's statement written down. It doesn't sound logical to hang around the city with the heat that's on Jordan right now, but you never know."

J.T. pushed back his chair, checked the map for directions to get to Lincoln Street, and left.

Bruce spoke up. "Boss, nobody answers at the All-Store facility. The website shows the place is only manned until five o'clock daily."

Tam heaved a deep sigh and rolled her neck. "All right, let's wait and see what the old lady has to say."

Chapter 43

J.T. knocked on the door of the modest, single-story house at 274 Lincoln Street. The porch light illuminated the stoop, where he stood and waited with his hands jammed deep into his pockets. A cool breeze swirled around his head and found its way down the unzipped jacket. J.T. shivered and pulled his collar up.

The curtain spread, and an old lady peeked out. J.T. flipped open the leather bifold that held his FBI identification and turned it toward her. She smiled and gave him a nod. A few seconds later, Edith Smart opened the door and welcomed him in.

"Thanks, ma'am, it's getting chilly outside. I'm Agent Harper, and I appreciate your call to the tip line." J.T. shook her hand. "A diligent person like you with watchful eyes sure does help us catch criminals."

She waved him to follow. "Let's sit in the kitchen and talk, agent. I just made some tea. That ought to warm you up."

J.T. walked with the woman, who appeared to be on the

high side of seventy. They passed through a short hallway and entered the kitchen. The square wooden table with two chairs sat below a window facing a small deck and the backyard.

"Have a seat, agent. How do you like your tea?"

"Black is fine, thank you, ma'am."

She placed two porcelain cups on matching saucers and set them on the table. The teapot was placed on a trivet between them, and she took a seat.

"Go ahead and help yourself."

J.T. gave her a thoughtful smile and poured tea for both of them. She reminded him of his grandma. "So what can you tell me about the white van, ma'am?"

"Well, it's not like I'm a snoop, but I do know the vehicles that belong in this neighborhood. I've lived in this house with mostly the same neighbors for twenty-seven years."

With his hands wrapped around the warm cup, J.T. took a sip and raised his brows for her to continue.

"I only noticed the van because I opened my drapes to let some light in and to see if today's paper was on the stoop. It was, so I went outside and grabbed it. The van was parked right across the street, and I know who lives in those homes. Nobody on that side of the street owns a vehicle like that. It looked... what's the word?"

"Raggedy, old, worn-out, beat-up?"

"Yeah, sort of worn, I'd say, and older. Not that I'm judging, mind you."

"I understand, ma'am. And you mentioned a missing hubcap?"

"Yes, that's right, on the driver's side rear wheel."

"Did you happen to see anyone in the vehicle? How about the model or a plate number?"

Edith scrunched her forehead. "Let me think about that. Oh, I did see someone at the back of the van for a split second. It looked like they grabbed a bag of some sort then walked away."

J.T. almost choked on his tea. "You saw somebody? Why didn't you mention that earlier?"

"Well, dear, I didn't actually see the person's face. I couldn't tell if it was a man or woman or if they were young or old. They wore jeans and a dark sweatshirt with the hood pulled up."

J.T.'s excitement was instantly deflated. His shoulders lowered with disappointment. "You couldn't even see their hair color?"

"Not with that hood over their head. They walked fast though and faced the ground, as if they had to get somewhere quickly."

"Or like they didn't want to be seen?"

She rubbed her chin then poured more tea. "Could be."

"Okay, how about size? Tall, short, heavy, or thin?"

"Man sized, I'd say, sort of like you."

J.T. gave that some thought. He knew anybody that described Jordan based on her size alone could easily mistake her for a man. "Did you see which way that person went?"

"I only saw them for a few seconds, and they went that way"—she pointed to her left—"on Lincoln. I brought the paper in the house, looked out the window again, and they were gone. I forgot all about the van until I saw the breaking news on TV. That's when I called the tip line and got ahold of you."

J.T. swallowed the last sip of his tea and stood. He thanked Edith for being a concerned citizen, shook her hand, and left his business card. "Please, give me a call if anything else comes to mind."

"I certainly will, Agent Harper. Drive carefully, now."

"Thank you, Mrs. Smart." J.T. pulled the collar up on his jacket and closed the door at his back.

Chapter 44

I've seen enough government cars to know that's definitely an FBI or police cruiser.

Jordan was coming up on the four-way stop at Lincoln Street when a black cruiser crossed through the intersection and continued on.

I need to get this van safely back in the garage.

Jordan made a rolling stop, flicked her cigarette out the window, and turned right. She looked in the rearview mirror and saw taillights disappear several blocks behind her. She turned left on Adams and pulled into the driveway.

I don't know what that was about, but if I need to leave again, I'll take Jeanie's car.

She pressed the button on Jeanie's remote and pulled into the garage then closed it behind her. She smiled as she passed the cinder blocks and entered the house.

Jordan turned toward Jeanie, still bound in the chair, as she entered the living room. The woman's chin rested against her chest.

"Hey, no dying on me." She ripped the tape off Jeanie's

mouth and slapped her cheek. "Wake up." She slapped her harder. "Damn you, wake up, I said."

Boozer came around the corner and rubbed against his owner's motionless leg. Jordan pushed him with her foot, and the cat hissed. "Get the hell out of here before I throw you outside."

The cat scampered down the hallway and disappeared into the first bedroom on the right. Jordan followed it and closed the door.

She heard Jeanie moan just as she was about to throw another glass of water on her. Jordan drank it instead.

"Good, you're still alive, but now I'll have to come up with something else that will keep you quiet. I wouldn't want the neighbors to know you have company."

Jeanie's head bobbed as she sucked in oxygen and looked around. "What happened to the agent?"

Jordan chuckled. "Best friends, are you? When did she have time to tell you her life story?"

Jeanie went silent.

"No matter, she's history now."

Jeanie's phone rang on the kitchen table. Her eyes darted in that direction as she pulled at her restraints.

"I wonder who that could be. Maybe I should check it out." Jordan disappeared around the corner and returned a minute later. She wore a grin that couldn't be hidden. "I listened to your voicemail, you know, in case it was something important. Looks like you're having company in the morning."

Fear crossed Jeanie's face, and tears wet her cheeks. "Jordan, I can explain."

"Shut up. You can't explain anything, and it's too late, anyway." Jordan loosened the paracord restraints. "Get up and put your hands behind your back."

Jeanie did as she was told, and Jordan zip-tied her wrists together.

"Sit down again so I can do your ankles."

Jeanie complied.

"There, you're free to move around as you please. You can shuffle forward. Your ankles are bound loosely. One scream and you die. No more questions, either, understand?"

"I understand."

Jordan turned Jeanie's phone to the vibrate mode and slid it into her back pocket. "Sit at the table. I'll make you something to eat."

Chapter 45

"Well?"

J.T. passed through the door of the command center with a deflated expression etched across his face. "I don't know, boss. It could go either way. The old lady wasn't senile or anything, so I have to take her at her word."

Agent Tam raised a questioning brow. "What does that mean?"

"She said she saw somebody at the back of the van but couldn't tell me if it was a man or woman. Apparently, whoever it was wore a dark hoodie and jeans. The hood was pulled up, and the person walked away at a quickened pace and carried a black bag. She did say the person was large. 'Man sized' were her actual words."

"Not much help there unless the van on the tape actually does have a missing back hubcap. Bruce, pull up the website for All-Store. See if there's a contact name and number for any of the locations. I don't care who answers. We need somebody to go to that facility and pull up the tape going back to last night."

Bruce planted himself at a computer and typed All-Store storage facility into the search bar. He found a nationwide listing, so he narrowed the search to Texas only.

"There are fourteen facilities in Texas, boss, with phone numbers but no names."

"Start calling all of them and see if anybody answers. You need to get a voice on the phone, a live one. No recordings."

J.T. stood in front of the oversized map of Houston, his arms folded across his chest, and stared at the streets.

"Something come to mind?" Agent Tam asked.

"The old lady said the person walked straight ahead of the van after they closed the back doors. I was just checking to see how far west Lincoln Street went and what streets intersect with it."

Tam studied the map with J.T. "Point out where Mrs. Smart lives."

J.T. tapped the map's surface. "Right there." He slid his finger west and followed Lincoln Street. "Lincoln only goes three blocks west before it turns into a frontage road along the freeway. There are two streets that intersect Lincoln, west of Mrs. Smart's house—Adams and Franklin—and they both go north and south. Why would anyone park a vehicle away from the house they lived at, or were visiting, instead of pulling into the driveway?"

"Good question unless they wanted to sneak up on the property owner."

"Exactly my point. All we need now is confirmation of that hubcap and we can start banging on doors. I doubt if anyone would walk beyond a five-block radius of their destination."

Tam turned toward Bruce. "How's it going on the phone calls?"

"I'm on number eleven, boss. So far nobody has answered at any of them."

Boardman checked the time and said it was 8:42. "Anybody up for coffee?"

The group nodded and got back to work. More calls came in, and more leads were checked out. Several detectives left to conduct interviews.

"Boss, I have someone on the line." Bruce held the receiver out, and Agent Tam crossed the room and pressed the button for speakerphone.

"Hello, this is Supervisory Special Agent Michelle Tam with the FBI. I have you on speakerphone. May I have your name and location, please?"

"This is Billy Brant, ma'am, and I'm at the Amarillo location."

"Thank you, Billy. I need to get somebody to the Houston facility on Collier Street. It's an emergency situation. Are you capable of doing that? We have to review a surveillance tape as soon as possible."

"One second, ma'am." Billy put Agent Tam on a brief hold. "Okay, it looks like that location has several people who take turns at the guard shack. Let me make a few calls. May I have a contact number?"

Tam rattled off the number and hung up. She heaved a hopeful sigh. "With any luck, we'll find out about that van tonight."

After a fifteen-minute wait during which Tam drank coffee and paced, the same phone rang again. Agent Tam picked it up. "Agent Michelle Tam speaking. How may I help you?"

"Ma'am, it's Billy Brant again."

"Yes, Billy. Please give me some good news."

"It is good news. Josh Lennart has agreed to help you with whatever you need at that location. He should be there in fifteen minutes, ma'am."

"I appreciate your help, Billy, and I'm going to put a good word in to the All-Store headquarters that you went above and beyond your duties to help out law enforcement. Thank you." Tam clicked off the call. "J.T. and I are heading out. Chief, do you want to accompany us?"

"Go ahead. I'll continue with the leads from here."

Tam and J.T. left the precinct and drove the twenty minutes to the All-Store location. Josh Lennart should have already arrived. The guard shack's light was illuminated—a good sign. With the cruiser parked along the driveway at the entrance, Tam knocked on the guard shack door, flashed her badge, and they were shown in. With the handshake and pleasantries out of the way, Tam told Josh exactly what they needed.

"Sure, no problem. I've never had the opportunity to help the FBI out before. It's kind of exciting."

J.T. gave the young man a pat on the shoulder. "Well, we certainly do appreciate you going out of your way, Josh."

"Okay, here we go. You need the tape that started yesterday, correct?"

"That's correct, but we need after nine p.m. going forward. We're looking for a white van with limousine tinted side windows," J.T. said.

Tam shook her head and groaned. "The van didn't show up on the tape until this morning. It came in and out several times, but I didn't write down the time. Start the tape at eight a.m. You can speed through it until we see movement then slow it down."

Josh slid the speed bar to the right and increased the footage to proceed in double time. They watched and waited.

"There! Okay, back it up a touch and slow it to normal speed. This is the first time we saw the van, but it did come in and out a few more times. We need to get an image of the back driver's side wheel, Josh. Pan in, pan out, but do whatever you can to get eyeballs on the entire driver's side."

"Will do, ma'am, but getting a side view of the entire vehicle from top to bottom won't be easy. Normally, the vehicles are entering and exiting, which only gives us a front and back image."

"How about when the van rounds the corner out of Row C?" J.T. asked.

"That could work if I zoom in as much as possible." Josh made a few adjustments, zoomed in, and sped up the footage to the time the van exited Row C.

"Bingo! Freeze that shot, Josh, and pull the image in the best you can." Tam looked at J.T. and grinned. "Son of a gun. No rear hubcap. I think it's time to start a knock and talk in Mrs. Smart's neighborhood."

They thanked Josh for his help, handed him their business cards, and took his information. They were back in the cruiser minutes later.

"Call the precinct and tell Boardman we need to establish a search perimeter around Mrs. Smart's address. Let him know we're on our way back."

Chapter 46

With a team of FBI agents, detectives, and officers in the command center, a perimeter was set up around Mrs. Smart's residence, with her home being ground zero. They would first make a drive-by sweep of the entire neighborhood and look for the white van parked along the street or in somebody's driveway. They agreed on an area within a five-block radius. If nothing popped, they would start a foot search and conduct a knock and talk at every house, going out two blocks in each direction.

"How many houses does that involve on foot?" Dave Miller asked.

"Unfortunately, a lot, Agent Miller," Chief Boardman said. "These homes were built after the Second World War when the housing boom took place. GIs got low-interest loans, and a lot of small two-bedroom homes were built in the area. I'm guessing we're looking at nearly seventy-five houses. The time of night doesn't help. The likelihood of anyone in this neighborhood, mostly elderly people or first-time home buyers with young kids, answering their doors after ten o'clock is slim to none. We'll probably be repeating our efforts tomorrow during daylight hours. It's closing in on ten p.m. already."

"Okay, let's do a thorough drive-by sweep of the area tonight and save the knock and talk for tomorrow starting at daybreak. I want the street name and address noted of every house that has a vehicle parked in the driveway."

"Ma'am?" an officer asked.

"You never know"—Agent Tam checked the name on his breast pocket—"Officer Jarvis. That van could be parked in someone's garage."

He nodded.

Agent Tam continued, "Since we have all night, we're doing a wider grid. I want a ten-block sweep in every direction and the vehicle-in-the-driveway information going out five blocks. Any questions?"

Nobody spoke up.

"Okay, let's assign areas and hit the streets. We'll reconvene here at four a.m. and see what we have."

The area was separated into seven grids, and teams of two were sent out in each cruiser. The neighborhoods were swept, slowly, methodically, and thoroughly.

At four a.m., with daybreak still hours away, each team reported back to the command center to reveal its findings. Two pots of much-needed coffee brewed while the results were tallied. Nobody had seen a white van parked along the search route, but thirty-seven homes in that five-block grid had cars parked in the driveway.

"Okay, that tells us which houses we'll go to first when

daylight breaks. The teams will remain the same for the knock and talks. Take your breaks now, grab a bite to eat, get some coffee in your systems, and we'll head out at dawn." Tam dropped down in her seat and cradled a coffee cup in her hands. She gave J.T. a long, concerned look. "What do you know about Jade's past history as a sergeant at the sheriff's department?"

"Not a lot except that she was a highly regarded and well-respected officer. Why?"

"Houston's police force and our FBI team are spending most of our waking hours and resources looking for her. Isn't this her first assignment out of your district?"

"It is, but SSA Spelling thought she was ready. She came highly recommended by SSA Dave Spencer in Quantico."

"Dave Spencer? How did she manage to become acquainted with him?"

"Dave and Jade's dad were good friends. Actually, Agent Spelling went to the police academy with Tom Monroe."

"Tom Monroe? He was Jade's father?"

J.T. nodded and took a sip of coffee. "That's quite a legacy to live up to, wouldn't you agree?"

"Absolutely. I had no idea. Still and all, once Jade is found, we have to get to the bottom of this. Agents can't go off halfcocked and take on a case by themselves. We're a team. The FBI doesn't tolerate solo players."

"Understood, ma'am, and I'm sure she's going to have a good explanation."

Tam drummed the tabletop with her fingertips then looked at the clock. "Get a few winks, J.T. We're heading out in two hours."

Chapter 47

I opened my eyes and had no idea where I was. The only thing I knew for sure was that I was wet, cold, and confused. I lay outside in the elements—that was a fact. Outlines of trees were taking shape as the vast night above me was giving way to dawn. Bugs found open spots around my jacket collar and pant legs, and I felt them crawling inside my clothes. I swatted things that skittered across my face, and my neck itched from bites. Crickets chirped and bullfrogs croaked in the distance. I knew I was near water. I also knew alligators inhabited Texas lakes and rivers. I had to get to dry land, and the sooner the better. My temples pounded as I tried to recall what happened and how I got to that spot. A lump had formed on the back of my head, but I couldn't remember why.

Slowly, I got to my hands and knees and assessed how I felt. I was dizzy, my head throbbed, and my body was chilled to the bone and badly bug bitten. I considered myself lucky. It could have been worse. I needed to get to my feet, figure out where I was, and find help.

Voices sounded in the distance. I was sure of it. The breaking light gave me opportunity to see a large body of water beyond the marsh grass. I forced myself to stand up, but I couldn't get close to the water's edge. The wet, soggy ground sucked my shoes in deeper with every movement I made. I wouldn't take a chance of stumbling over a well-hidden venomous snake or a hungry alligator.

Squinting might help me see better. It felt as if my eyes were coated with a foggy film. I stared at the calm, glasslike water and hoped to see something move—something human.

The noise sounded again. I knew it wasn't birdcalls or the wind. It was conversation and laughter, and it echoed across the water.

I yelled out for help and was shocked at the sound of my own voice. Raspy, raw noises came from deep within my throat. Lying all night in the damp cold probably caused it, but I couldn't waste the only opportunity I had to get rescued. I heard them again and finally saw what I had prayed for. In the distance, two men paddled a rowboat across the water. I waved my arms and yelled as loud as I could to get their attention even though my throat felt as if I had swallowed barbed wire.

The man sitting at the bow pointed toward me. I waved again and called out for help. They turned the rowboat toward shore and headed in my direction. I thanked God for answering my prayers.

"What in the world?" The man at the bow shielded his eyes and got a better look at me.

"Help me, please. I need to get out of here. I'm an FBI agent, and I believe I was drugged. I woke up out here in the marsh. Please, I need to use a phone."

"Can you get to the pier?"

"I have no idea where that is. How far? Which way?"

"I can see it from here, ma'am. There's a dirt path behind you about fifty feet. Go left on that path for one hundred yards or so. You'll see a sign with an arrow pointing toward the water. The pier is right there. We'll meet you there with the boat."

"Thank you so much. I'll be fine as soon as I get out of this muck and on dry ground. I think I've lost one of my shoes, but I'll try to hurry."

The tangle of marsh grasses tripped me as I plowed through the mess. I finally hit dry ground, kicked off the remaining shoe that weighed me down with mud, and stumbled forward on the path. My head pounded with each step. I reached the sign and turned left. The pier was directly ahead, and the men were only twenty feet out. I watched my footing as I made my way down the wooden structure and grabbed the rope they threw to me. With the rowboat against the pier and the rope safely secured to a post, the men climbed out and joined me. They stared at me as if I was the creature from the Black Lagoon, and I'm sure I looked the part.

"Thank you so much. You have no idea what your help means to me."

"Ma'am, are you really an FBI agent?"

"I'm sure I don't look like one at the moment, but yes,

I am. My name is Jade Monroe, and you are?" I held out my damp hand.

The man that had been sitting at the bow introduced himself as Leon Winkler, and his friend was Dan Carlisle. They said they were retired and out to do some Sunday morning fishing.

"I'm so thankful you happened along. Where in the world am I?"

"This is Sheldon Lake State Park, and you were damn lucky to be found at all. This is a 2,800-acre park, and not many people are out here in the cooler months. Speaking of cooler, you're shaking. You have to be freezing. Take my coat. At least it's dry."

"Thank you, Leon." I slipped his flannel-lined jacket over my stiff, wet shoulders.

"Are those what I think they are?" Dan pointed at my neck.

Instinctively, I touched the multiple spots where I had been zapped with the stun gun. Until that moment, I had forgotten all about them. The cobwebs in my mind began to clear as the Methohexital wore off and the images of Jordan returned.

I nodded in response then asked to use a phone.

"Here you go, Jade," Dan said. "Use mine."

At that moment, I couldn't recall anyone's phone number except my mom's. It was still the same number she'd had when we were kids living at home. I dialed it.

"Hello. If this is a telemarketing call on a Sunday morning, you should be ashamed."

"Mom, it's Jade."

"Jade, oh my God, honey, we've been worried sick."

"Mom, I need you to listen carefully to my every word. It's imperative you call Jack the second we hang up. You do have his number, don't you?"

"Well, it's somewhere around here."

"Never mind. Call Amber, then. Don't dillydally, just call her now and tell her to contact Agent Harper immediately. Have her tell him I'm safe and at Sheldon Lake State Park. Write this phone number down." I gave her Dan's number. "Have Agent Harper call this number right away. Do you have everything I just said?"

"Yes, honey. Call Amber, tell her to call Agent Harper, and give him the phone number you just rattled off."

"Good. Do it now. I'll be expecting his call in five minutes. I love you, Mom. Goodbye."

Leon shook his head, as if in disbelief. "You don't remember anything about how you ended up here?"

"It's coming back to me. I'm sure I was drugged and left here to die. I can't go into details, but you'll see something on the news in the next day or so, I guarantee it."

Leon climbed down to the boat, grabbed his tackle box and a thermos, and brought them up. "I got something for you, Jade."

I gave him a weak smile. "I hope it isn't worms."

"Nope, no worms." He grinned. "But I always carry trail mix with me. Here, have some." He twisted the cap off the thermos and poured steaming coffee into it. "Here you go. You look like you can use something hot to drink too."

I held the warm cap between my hands and sipped the coffee. "This is good, thanks."

"It's quite a walk back to the entrance, Jade. You're better off climbing in the boat with us and cutting across the water." Leon looked down at my feet. "Barefoot? That would take a while."

"Sounds like a good idea. How far is downtown from here?"

"Downtown is a half hour southwest, unless you're in law enforcement. I'm sure they can make it in twenty minutes."

"How long will it take to get back to where you parked your vehicle?"

"About the same amount of time. Let's head out now, and you can hang onto my phone. No reason to wait on the pier for your call," Dan said.

"Okay, I'm ready whenever you guys are."

Leon helped me into the rowboat, and Dan untied the rope, climbed in, and pushed us back with an oar. They turned the boat around, and we headed to the launch and parking lot area. Within minutes, Dan's phone rang. I checked the screen and knew if it was J.T., he'd block the call to a civilian's phone. The call was blocked. Dan nodded the go-ahead, and I cautiously answered with a simple *hello*.

"Jade, is that really you?"

"J.T.?"

I heard a familiar laugh, then a groan, then several curse words. "All I need to know is your location. The rest we'll deal with later. We're east of the city right now, trying to pinpoint where Jordan is hunkered down."

"I think I can help speed up that process, but first come and get me. I'll be at the boat launch in Sheldon Lake State Park."

"You got it. Give me a sec."

I heard J.T. yelling to someone, then he came back to the phone. "Okay, we're fifteen minutes from you. The cavalry is coming, partner. Stay put and take a breath."

I hung up and handed the phone to Dan. My personal nightmare with Jordan was over. Hopefully it wasn't too late for Jeanie. I wiped my eyes with gratitude and thanked my new friends for rescuing me.

"Here we are," Dan said.

They rowed the boat until we reached the cement launch area, then Leon climbed out. He grabbed the rope and tied it to a tree. Dan and I climbed out after him. Several picnic tables lined the parking lot. We sat and waited.

"I'm working out of the FBI field office in Houston. I'm hoping this case will be wrapped up in a day or two so I can go home."

"Where's home?" Dan asked.

I smiled then chuckled. "Just north of Milwaukee, Wisconsin."

Leon shrugged. "You mean the arctic tundra? Just thinking of those long winters makes me shiver."

"After living there my entire life, I'm finally making peace with it." I heard the sounds of sirens approaching then saw the red and blues flash on two squad cars and two black sedans as they skidded into the parking lot. I grinned. "Looks like the cavalry is here."

J.T. and Agent Tam jumped out of the first cruiser and ran to me. Dave and Bruce were right behind them.

"Jade, are you okay? Do you need an ambulance?" J.T. yelled out orders to the police officers.

"I'm okay, just a bit weak."

"Let's get this park searched," Agent Tam called out.

"Ma'am, don't bother. I don't think Jordan spent any time here other than finding a good dump spot for me. These two men are my guardian angels, and I don't know if I would have found my way out of here without them."

J.T. and Agent Tam shook Leon and Dan's hands as I introduced them.

"Jade, you should still be checked over. You look terrible," Tam said.

"I think most everything will wash off with a hot shower. How about giving me an hour to clean up and eat, then I think I can track down Jordan and end this once and for all."

I asked J.T. to give Dan and Leon his card as a contact until I got another phone. I wanted to thank them properly before we headed back to Milwaukee. With hugs of gratitude, I thanked my heroes and got in the car. We headed to the hotel so I could clean up.

Chapter 48

Jeanie sat in the same chair as last night, once again wrapped in red paracord. The silver duct tape stretched across her mouth kept her quiet. Her chair faced the front door, and a vacant chair sat next to it. Jordan pulled every curtain closed on the street side of the house then patiently waited on the couch and stared at Jeanie's phone. A text would surely come in any minute to say when her guest would arrive.

Jordan sipped coffee while her eyes darted from the phone, to Jeanie, then back to the phone. "Oh, I almost forgot. Where is my brain right now?"

She leaped off the couch and disappeared around the corner. The garage door sounded as it opened and closed—twice. Minutes later, Jordan carried a cinder block into the living room, left again, then brought in a second one.

"There, might as well have everything ready to go." She took her seat again and leaned over the phone. "Awesome, a text came in." She picked up the phone, swiped it with her index finger, and read the text. She chuckled and responded then threw the phone on the coffee table. "It's almost show time."

Jeanie squirmed on the chair. It teetered precariously to the point of nearly falling over.

"Knock it off. Sit still and accept your fate. It will be over with soon enough."

With her arm over the back of the couch, Jordan separated the curtain with her index finger just enough to see the driveway. She'd need a minute to prepare. Blitz attacks were her specialty. A wide grin spread across her face, and she crossed the room to stand in front of Jeanie. She leaned in, inches from Jeanie's face. "He's here."

With her necessities out of the backpack and ready to go, Jordan stood behind the front door and waited. She heard footsteps on the porch, then she watched as the doorknob jiggled when he unlocked it. Her thumb rested against the stun gun's red button. He pushed the door open.

"Hey, babe, why is your car parked in the driveway? What in God's name?"

He barely had enough time to get the words out of his mouth before he was hit with the stun gun. Jordan laid into it and pressed it deep against his neck. A loud grunt sounded, he twitched, and with a hard thud, he hit the ground. Jeanie screamed through the tape and rocked the chair. In a split second, Jordan had crossed the room and backhanded her with such force that the chair tipped backward and crashed to the floor.

Jeanie's issues were secondary. He needed to be restrained quickly before he came to his senses. Jordan rolled him over and kneed his back to hold him down. She grabbed his arms and zip-tied them tightly. He was waking up. As she held the longest zip tie with her teeth, she pushed up his pant legs, grabbed the tie, and secured his ankles together. She gave the plastic restraint an extra hard pull. With the most important part done, she rolled him again to face her.

The realization hit him as he stared into her eyes. "Jordan?"

She coiled back her fist, punched him in the face, battered him into unconsciousness, then ripped a length of tape off the roll and spread it across his mouth. Jordan struggled to drag his dead weight across the room. With a heave, she propped him up in the chair next to Jeanie and bound him with paracord.

Chapter 49

I felt human again. The dirt and bugs had been washed down the shower drain. I put on a clean pair of clothes then exited my room and took the elevator to the first floor, where J.T. waited in the hotel lobby.

"That's more like it. You look way less scary than before."

I didn't know J.T. as well as Jack, so the punch in the arm I would have given him would be saved for the future.

"Let's hit the drive-through so you can eat on the way."

"But the field office is just down the street."

"That's right, you don't know. We set up a command center at the downtown police department yesterday so everyone could combine their efforts to find you and Jordan. There's a lot you don't know."

"And a lot you don't, either. Let's get Jordan first and worry about explanations later."

J.T. pulled up to the ordering board. "What would you like?"

"Two egg sandwiches, an order of hash browns, and a large coffee."

"You sure that's enough?"

"Okay, make it two hash browns."

J.T. placed the order, and I wolfed down the food as he drove. "At least my pounding headache is going away. I'm not sure if it was from the Methohexital or when I hit the floor with the back of my head."

"You could have suffered a concussion, Jade."

"I know, but apparently I'm okay. I couldn't have stayed awake last night, anyway, since I was drugged. Jordan is really off her rocker, J.T. That woman, Jeanie, was in bad shape when I saw her."

"The command center is set up with search parameters on the map. Let's see if that area jogs anything in your mind."

"I don't have a phone anymore, J.T. Jordan stomped it, and she has my sidearm too."

"Great. Not only is she a wack job, she's an armed one."

We arrived at the downtown police department at eight thirty and entered the command center. Tam and Boardman stood at the head of the table. A smile crossed Tam's face.

"Agent Monroe, you look human again. Are you sure you're okay to participate?"

"I am, ma'am, and I know we can expedite finding Jordan with my help. May I?"

She nodded.

I approached the map and studied the search grid. An inner and outer ring was formed with red pushpins with Lincoln Street running through the center.

"Okay, what am I looking at?"

Boardman pointed at the outer ring. "We searched within that area last night for Jordan's white van. No results."

"And the inner ring?"

J.T. spoke up. "That's the location we searched and documented of all the houses that had a car parked in the driveway."

I nodded. "Very smart. And according to the eyewitness you told me about, J.T., Jordan's van was parked where?"

He poked the map on the east side of Lincoln Street. "Right here, against the curb, facing west."

I sat at the table and rubbed my forehead in thought. "I need a piece of paper and a pen."

Boardman grabbed them out of a cupboard near the door and handed them to me. "Here you go, Jade."

"Thanks, sir. Okay, Jordan had me tied up on the floor of the van, but I could see out the side windows. It felt like she turned around on the street, pulled over to the curb, and parked. I remember seeing several street signs through the window as she passed them. A big mistake on her part for not blindfolding me."

"Makes sense," Agent Tam said. "That's when she pulled a U-turn on Lincoln Street." Tam poured me a cup of coffee as I focused on what I remembered.

"Thank you, ma'am." I looked at the map again. "Yeah, here we go. I saw the street signs at the intersections of Franklin and Adams, here, and here," I jabbed the map with my index finger then sat back down and sketched out what I remembered. "Jordan turned around and parked, so the van was here." I drew an *X* on the paper beyond the two intersections with Lincoln Street. "She left me alone for a while, but when she came back, she got in and drove ahead for twenty seconds or so and made a left. It only took a few seconds more before we turned left again into a driveway. She stopped, I heard the sound of a garage door opening, and then she pulled in and closed the overhead."

Dave stared at my drawing. "That means the house you were at is on Adams Street and on the left. Do you remember if it was a one-car garage or two?"

"It definitely was a one-car garage and crowded inside."

Boardman spoke up. "Who has the records of the houses with cars in the driveway?"

"They're right here, sir." Officer Colby pushed the five stapled sheets of paper across the table.

Boardman flipped the sheets until he saw an address for Adams Street. "Colby, grab a computer and pull up the street view of Adams Street. I need to know how far in is 331 Adams and which side of the street it's on."

"Nailed it, boss, and 331 Adams is the fourth house on the left."

I jumped from my chair. "We have to go. There's no time to waste."

"One second, Jade. Colby, pull up the name locator app and type in that house number. I need to know who lives there."

"The app just spit out the name Jeanie Livingston." Colby turned toward me with a raised brow.

"That's her. I need a weapon. Jordan took mine."

"Jade, you need to sit this one out. We can handle it," Agent Tam said.

"With all due respect, ma'am, there's no way in hell I'm sitting this one out after all the crap Jordan put me through." J.T. grinned, and I felt my face flush. "Besides, I know the layout of the house, and I'm a familiar face to Jeanie, that is, if she's still alive."

"Okay, somebody get Agent Monroe a weapon. Let's roll."

Chapter 50

"Finally waking up? Hell, Jeanie is tougher than you are, Kent. How does it feel to literally lose control?" She smirked and glanced at the wet spot between his legs. "You're pathetic. You can't help your whore girlfriend, you can't lie to me anymore, and you can't call the shots. I'm in charge now."

Jordan watched from across the room, comfortable on the couch, as Kent stared at Jeanie's swollen face and frantic eyes.

"She isn't that pretty anymore, is she? But then you look like a pile of shit too."

He thrashed in the chair.

She cocked her head. His anguish amused her. "Is there something you want to say?"

He nodded.

Jordan pushed off the couch and approached them then ripped the tape and a layer of skin off his lips. Kent groaned, and he grimaced with pain.

"What the hell is wrong with you? Have you lost your mind?"

She laughed and gave him a violent slap across the face. Jordan pulled Jade's gun out of her pocket and rubbed the cold steel barrel against Kent's reddened cheek. He jerked his head back.

"No, Kent, I didn't lose my mind. Just my daughter. Imagine my surprise, a week ago today as a matter of fact, on the sixth-month anniversary of Emily's death. You thought I'd already left to go shopping, but I forgot the grocery list. When I came back into the house, I overheard you talking on your phone in the bedroom." Jordan stuck her finger in Jeanie's face and jabbed her. She spat the words at both of them. "You were talking to this pig right here, the woman that used to be my best friend. You were discussing *our* daughter and how, six months later, you still hadn't gotten over your feeling of guilt. I heard you admit how you weren't watching her when the wall collapsed. Instead, you were on the phone, professing your love for Jeanie and planning your next sexcapade. Emily was outside by herself, and both of you killed her, just as much as the men who designed and built that faulty wall, and just as much as John Nels did when he gave all of those people a pass and refused to sue them." Jordan wiped her tear-stained cheeks on her sleeve. "How many miscarriages did I endure before we finally got that gift, our precious Emily, and now she's gone?"

"Jordan, please, it was a horrible accident."

"No, it wasn't. She wouldn't be dead if you would have been paying attention to her instead of talking to your girlfriend on the phone. Emily was only three years old, for God's sake. It's time."

"Time for what?"

"Time to pay for your deception. You cheated on me with my best friend, and you killed our daughter, the only child I'll ever have. Look where you are right now, Kent. When I talked to you on the phone last night, you said you'd be home this morning. I guess you meant *after* you stopped in for a quickie with Jeanie. You have no remorse." Jordan followed Kent's eyes as he locked on the blocks that sat against the wall. She laughed. "Look familiar? Yeah, those are the cinder blocks from our house. I only need two. One for each of you."

Jordan picked them up, one at a time, and placed them next to each chair. Kent pleaded and begged for mercy.

"You know, I've listened to you far too long. Always criticizing me, always telling me I should be medicated. I've heard enough." She leaned in, close enough to feel his breath on her skin, and stretched the tape over his mouth. "There, I never want to hear your voice again."

She turned Jeanie's chair so it would line up against the back of Kent's. She unwound the roll of duct tape as she circled them twice and bound them together.

"Sorry you can't gaze into each other's eyes as you die, but that's life. Or not." She chuckled as she tore the tape off the roll. "There, that's perfect." Jordan stood back and studied her work. "You killed Emily together, now you can die together. Which do you want first, the cinder block crushing your skull or a bullet to the brain?"

Chapter 51

We came in quickly and quietly. The sirens had been silenced two miles back, and now the house was surrounded. Squad cars had blocked off Adams, Lincoln, and Franklin Streets. Three black sedans, two cruisers, and an ambulance filled the street to the left of Jeanie Livingston's home as we gathered along the side of the house and planned our approach.

"Did you find out who that second car in the driveway belongs to?" I whispered out over my radio. Officer Colby had pulled up the plate number for that mystery vehicle on his squad car's computer.

"Yes, Agent Monroe. That vehicle belongs to Kent Taylor."

"Shit. That's Jordan's husband. What about the garage?"

Boardman responded. "We have eyes on the white van, Jade. It's parked inside."

"Okay, guys, I'm taking the front door with J.T., Dave, and Bruce. The side door back there"—I pointed over my shoulder—"leads into the laundry room, which is attached to the kitchen. We need several officers to breach that door.

There's an entry into a mudroom from the garage, but that probably won't be an issue since the overhead is closed. The last entry point is the patio sliders at the back, but we should hold off on that one until the last second. We don't know where they're located in the house just yet, and we don't want her to see any of us. This has to be a blitz attack, and don't forget she has my gun. From our initial drive-by, it looked like all the curtains were drawn. That'll help us sneak up on the house. Everyone have your ears perked. I'll give the signal right as we breach the front door." I tapped my chest. "Protected?"

The officers nodded. They were all wearing vests.

"Okay, this woman is a loose cannon. Be careful."

I jerked my head to the left, crouched down, and ran for the front door with J.T., Dave, and Bruce at my side. We reached the stoop, positioned ourselves, then I whispered into my radio. "Let's do it!"

With a nod from J.T. and our guns drawn, I coiled back my leg and, with a forceful kick, broke in the door.

Jordan stood in front of Kent and Jeanie with a cinder block high above her head. She spun at the sound behind her.

"Jordan Taylor, drop that block now or I'll shoot!"

Jordan laughed when she saw me. "Agent Monroe, you must have nine lives. I certainly didn't think I'd see you again."

"I told you to drop that cinder block."

Kent rocked the chairs, and his eyes bulged with fear. Jordan's concentration on me broke when the chairs tipped and fell to the floor. She yelled out and raised the block even higher and was ready to release it into their skulls with a fury. I had a split second to think and shot the cinder block. It exploded in her hands. Gravel dust and pieces of cement shot out like shrapnel, and that second of commotion gave Jordan just enough time to react. I saw the gun come out of her pocket. Three shots rang out—two in the heads of Kent and Jeanie and one from Bruce's weapon that went into Jordan's chest.

J.T. ran out to the sidewalk. "Son of a bitch, get the EMTs in here, now."

Everyone rounded the house to see what had taken place. The ambulance backed across the front lawn, and the EMTs pulled out a gurney.

"Step aside and let us through."

"What the hell happened in here?" Tam yelled out as she barged into the living room.

I knelt at Jeanie and Kent's lifeless bodies. There was nothing anyone could do to help them, that much was obvious. I turned to Tam and shook my head.

"What about Jordan?"

I touched her neck and found a weak pulse. I waved the EMTs over. "Hurry, guys, she's still breathing."

Jordan was stabilized for the moment and loaded into the ambulance. The EMT closed the back doors.

"Hang on," I said and stepped up on the bumper. "I'm riding with her."

J.T. gave me a questioning look. "Why, Jade?"

"She doesn't look like she has long for this life. I need more from her."

I climbed in, slammed the doors, and the ambulance hit the sirens.

"Jordan, can you hear me?"

She groaned, and bubbles of blood seeped out of her mouth.

"Jordan, talk to me. Tell me why you snapped."

"Kent."

"What about Kent?"

"He let Emily die… not watching her." Jordan coughed out a mouthful of blood. "He was on the phone with Jeanie instead."

Piece by piece, the story came together. I understood, even as deluded as she was, why she thought the killings were deserved.

"Why did you kill Beverly Grant, the 9-1-1 operator? What was her sin?"

Jordan sucked in a deep breath, and her raspy voice trailed off.

"Jordan? Why did Bev Grant die?"

Blood pooled on the gurney beneath Jordan, and I knew she didn't have long. Her words were barely a whisper. I leaned in as close as I could, my ear against her bloody lips.

"She sent the ambulance to the wrong address. Emily might have lived if the EMTs had gotten there ten minutes earlier. Instead, my baby died in the ambulance just like—"

"Just like what, Jordan? Just like what?"

A deep and final breath came from her mouth, almost like a sigh of relief. The demons had left her body. I pulled back and looked at Jordan's face. Her eyes were fixed and unblinking. I checked her pulse and put my ear to her chest. She was gone.

I knocked on the window between me and the driver's cab. The EMT in the passenger seat turned around, and I shook my head. I saw him slide up his sleeve and check the time. The driver pulled to the curb, and they came around the back. They needed to double-check for a pulse and officially call the time of her death. Jordan Taylor died at 10:42 Sunday morning. The EMT silenced the siren and drove her body to the hospital's morgue.

Chapter 52

"About ready to head out?" J.T. asked.

"Yeah, just bang on my door in twenty minutes. I'll know it's you." I hung up and finished packing.

Our paperwork and debriefing was complete, and the case in Houston was closed. Tam needed a good explanation of why I had gone to the Taylor house alone that night. I explained to her how I had tried J.T.'s phone numerous times as I drove but wasn't able to get through to him. Although we never learned why—whether it was cell service issues, something blocking the reception when the guys were at TaTas, or a hundred other reasons—the fact remained that I went to Jordan's house alone and suffered the consequences.

Jordan's trigger, I learned in her ambulance confession, was that on the sixth-month anniversary of Emily's death, she found out Kent and Jeanie were having an affair. She also overheard Kent admit his guilt about not keeping his eye on Emily that fateful day.

As sad as the situation was, Jordan lost control and

snapped. She turned into a violent serial killer, and she had to be stopped.

When it was all said and done, Jordan Taylor, along with eight other people, died because of a tragic accident that had happened six months prior. I'd never understand the demons that took over the mind of a serial killer, but my duty as a sworn FBI agent was to find them, apprehend them if at all possible, and bring them to justice.

J.T. and I had said our goodbyes to Agent Tam, Bruce, and Dave earlier that morning. Now, our jet was fueled and waiting on the tarmac for takeoff in an hour.

I zipped my suitcase and gave myself a final glance in the mirror. I was thankful for concealer to cover the stun gun marks and bruises until they were healed.

A loud bang sounded on my door. I looked through the peephole and saw J.T. grinning, then he covered the hole with his finger. I chuckled and opened the door.

"Spying on me, huh, partner?"

"Who, me?"

"Yeah, right." He stretched out his hand and took my bag. "Ready to go home?"

"Definitely."

The elevator doors opened at the first floor. We checked out at the reception counter and turned to the exit when I saw two familiar faces walking toward me.

I laughed as I embraced both of them. "I can't believe you guys recognized me."

Dan and Leon smirked. "We had to stop by. We were curious."

"Yeah? About what?"

"We were pretty sure there was a good-looking FBI agent under the dirt and bug bites, and we were right."

I gave them each a kiss on the cheek. "If I didn't know better, I'd say you old farts are flirting with me. In all sincerity, you guys are my heroes, and I'll always be grateful for your help."

Leon looked at our suitcases. "Heading home, Jade?"

"I'm afraid so. Wisconsin is looking pretty good right now. Take care, guys, and stay out of mischief unless you're saving someone's life."

I waved goodbye to the guys as J.T. and I climbed into the waiting car. We were at the airport and sitting on the jet forty-five minutes later.

"I'm going to give Spelling a call and tell him we're on the plane. We'll update the group in the morning. Tonight, I just want to go home, relax with a bulldog on my lap, and kick up my feet."

"I feel ya, partner." I clicked my seat belt and stared out the window. It had been a long week, and I looked forward to going home too.

The engines revved, the jet thrusted forward, and we took to the sky.

"I still have time to call Amber, don't I?"

"Yeah, another few minutes."

I dialed my sister and told her we were heading back. I promised I'd be home for dinner. Amber said meatloaf, mashed potatoes, gravy, and corn were on that night's menu.

"It sounds delicious, sis, and I can't wait. Just one more thing. I'd love a large glass of wine when I get home, and pour one for yourself, Jack, and Kate too. I need a comfy chair, a fire in the fireplace, and my feet on the ottoman. We have a lot of catching up to do."

THE END

Thank you for reading *Snapped*, Book 1 in the new Agent Jade Monroe FBI Thriller Series. I hope you enjoyed it!

Follow the complete Jade Monroe saga starting with the Detective Jade Monroe Crime Thriller Series. The books are listed in order below:

Maniacal
Captive
Fallacy
Premonition
Exposed

Stay abreast of my new releases by signing up for my VIP email list at: http://cmsutter.com/newsletter/

You'll be one of the first to get a glimpse of the cover reveals and release dates, and you'll have a chance at exciting raffles and freebies offered throughout the series.

Posting a review will help other readers find my books. I appreciate every review, whether positive or negative, and if you have a second to spare, a review is truly appreciated.

Again, thank you for reading!

Visit my author website at: http://cmsutter.com/

See all of my available titles at:
http://cmsutter.com/available-books/

Made in the USA
Monee, IL
29 March 2021